THE GUNS OF SANTA SANGRE

THE GUNS OF SANTA SANGRE

ERIC RED

SHORT, SCARY TALES PUBLICATIONS

BIRMINGHAM, ENGLAND

ISBN: 978-1-909640-91-7

2017 SST Publications Trade Hardcover Edition

Published by
Short, Scary Tales Publications
15 North Roundhay
Birmingham
B33 9PE
England

www.sstpublications.co.uk

Book design by Paul Fry

Printed in the United States of America and the United Kingdom

First Edition: March 2017

10 9 8 7 6 5 4 3 2 1

To my grandmother, Meg "Mimi" Wilson,
whose love and support will last me a lifetime,
and Spunky, my little werewolf.

Other Books in **Eric Red's The Men Who Walk Like Wolves** Series

The Wolves of El Diablo – *Coming 2017*
The Claws of Rio Muerta – *Coming 2018*

THE GUNS OF SANTA SANGRE

CHAPTER ONE

JOHN WHISTLER RECKONED HE WAS WITHIN THIRTY miles of the wanted men when they lost the wheel. Now the stagecoach was out of commission, the bounty hunter stranded to hell in the bowels of the Mexican desert, with nobody but two damn do-nothing stage drivers and the Sonoma rental wench. It was the gloaming, the sky getting dark, but the edge was off the terrible heat so he figured they'd picked a good time to break down as any.

The big mustached man in duster and ten-gallon hat stood impatiently rotating and clicking the cylinder of his Colt Dragoon pistol about two hundred feet from the disabled wagon. Whistler stared out at the forbidding, craggy Durango canyon country and vast canopy of turquoise- and purple- and rose-streaked late evening sky. He listened to the two Wells Fargo men arguing and cussing and the sounds of banging and creaking as the men finished the repairs on the broken slats of the right rear wheel they were fitting back into place. The weathered brown carriage was tilted at an obtuse angle. The team of four horses stood bored in their harness at the front of the chassis, tails flitting at flies.

Whistler looked over to where the sweat-soaked fifteen-year-old prostitute in the black velvet corset and petticoat stood fanning herself.

She winked at him. Eyes of violet, red hair spilling down her shoulders, she smelt sweetly of rose water and sex. Her name she'd told him was Daisy and she had herself a going concern riding the stage line back and forth, servicing passengers and kicking back a few bucks to the driver. A sweet little set up. The whore had been knee to knee with him the whole trip from Sonoma in the cramped and jouncing stage, bouncing pale freckled breasts spilling out of her corset a few feet from his face on the opposite seat. The first ten got him a blowjob. Another twenty got her to hike up her petticoats and the bump of the stage did the work for him.

The bounty hunter took out his silver pocket watch on the chain from his vest and snapped it open. The name "John Whistler" was engraved in elegant lettering inside the lid. The hands of the clock read 7:53. Annoyed at being behind schedule, the man gruffly closed the watch and pocketed it.

The stagecoach junction was supposed to be just twenty miles from here, the old driver told him. Damn bit of luck. Whistler would have been there already, should have made it by dusk but for the stage mishap. Hell, he had those bad men he hunted dead to rights. They might not be there tomorrow morning. No matter, he was right on their ass and would catch up with them soon enough. The bounty hunter took out the folded wanted poster in his pocket and regarded it. The crudely sketched faces of the three outlaws stared back at him from the crumpled paper in the red hue of twilight.

Samuel Tucker.

John Fix.

Lars Bodie.

Notorious names in bold block-type lettering just above the $1,000.00 reward notice on each of their heads. Gunfighters and killers with lots of bodies strewn in their wake. These men were good, but he was better. The bounty hunter had gotten his lead on their current whereabouts from a Mexican ramrod who had seen them just the evening before in a small outpost thirty miles east from where Whistler now stood. The trail was coming to an end. Their bodies would be slung over saddles. Or his would.

He'd be out of Mexico one way or the other. He drew and admired his Smith & Wesson Scofield .45. It had no trigger guard. Made it faster to draw and fire unimpeded by such inconveniences. A saguaro cactus sat like an upright fork a few hundred yards away, the tines poking black spokes against the glowing rust of the end of the day. He contemplated a little target practice on the plant to kill the time, but reckoned he better save his bullets. The formidable men he was hunting knew how to place theirs.

Mostly, he just wanted the hell out of Mexico.

From the sound of things behind him, they were getting that wheel fixed, and it was about time. He turned around to see the fat, bearded stage driver and his young Mexican shotgunner in the scarf and vest tightening the bolts on the displaced wagon wheel and using wrenches to adjust the torque on the axle. Any time now they'd be back on the road. But he'd lost a day.

"How you boys doing on that wheel?" Whistler called over.

"It's repaired, but you best settle in, mister," the old stage driver grumbled. "Because we're here for the night and pulling out at dawn."

"That does not suit me."

"It doesn't matter. We're not driving this stage in the dark, not through this kind of terrain."

"But—"

"There be cliffs and ruts and ravines everywhere along the trail 'twixt here and the junction and the stage could take a plunge with one wrong turn."

The four people grouped by the carriage in the failing light.

A huge full moon hung in the sky, clouded with haze.

They heard the wolves.

Not like any Whistler heard before. A keening, yipping lupine chorus came from all sides out in the canyons. The howls began low but rose in strident pitch and timbre until they became a high shrieking bay. It was a sound to freeze your blood. The bounty hunter looked at the stage driver, who was looking at the Mexican guard with the shotgun, who seemed like he was about to soil himself.

"Coyotes?" Whistler asked, staring out into the near total darkness that began about three hundred feet from where they stood. The desert spaces that in daylight spread so vast were now claustrophobic and invisible beyond. The full moon was high and bright, obstructed by clouds and oddly cast no light. A tiny trickle of moonlight showed a crag of mountain peak in the gloom.

"Sure," said the old Wells Fargo guy.

"*Niente,*" whispered the guard.

"What then?"

The guard didn't answer.

The big wolves, or whatever they were, roared in unison, a sonic garrote of cacophonic sound tightening around them. Closing in. The hooker was shivering in fear, her eyes huge as her dainty hands covered her ears against the bellowing growls. "Something's out there. We got to get out of here," she whimpered.

"I'm with her," Whistler said, confronting the driver. "We best be on our way directly."

The old timer threw down, yelling in the bounty hunter's face, spattering saliva. "I told you tain't driving this rig at night on this trail or the stagecoach will crash because I cain't see for shit!"

By now the four horses were starting to panic, pawing the ground with their hooves, long snouts whipping back and forth in their bridles and bits, eyes like marbles and ears pinned back at the horrific music in the hills.

The monstrous roaring echoing around the canyons continued unabated and drew nearer and nearer. The guard, pale and face pouring with sweat, started babbling to the driver in Spanish, and the old man yelled back at him in the local tongue that Whistler barely understood. One thing was obvious. The Mexican knew what those sounds belonged to and wanted out of there. The argument became a shoving match, and the younger man won, clambering desperately up into the driver's bench by the luggage roof rack, grabbing the reins and gesturing madly for the bounty hunter and the hooker to get into the stagecoach and hurry it up.

"After you, ma'am," quipped Whistler to the tart. He opened the door and eased her into the carriage with a helpful hand up her skirt on her firm rear end. Then he put his boot on the metal step and climbed in across from her.

"Shit!" swore the old Wells Fargo driver, climbing up onto the driver's seat and cursing the whole way. He shoved the guard aside, grabbing the reins. "I'm drivin'," he shouted, "you'll put us in a damn ditch. YYEEEE—AHHH!" He cracked the reins and the team surged forward, the stagecoach pulling out.

The carriage picked up speed, scared horses hauling the rig at a full gallop. The wagon rocked back and forth on the uneven terrain as it plunged into the desert nocturne. Whistler could still hear the howling, but they seemed to be moving away from it. All he heard were the sounds of the wooden wheels on the rocks, the squeaking of the chassis suspension and the loud pounding of the hooves. He looked across from him in the tight, trembling quarters to see the hooker frozen in the leather seat a few feet away, pale fragile face staring out the open window of the stagecoach, eyes bugging out.

"Hurry, hurry . . ." she murmured.

The big wolves bayed.

And gave chase.

The bounty hunter drew both pistols and gripped them in his fists, looking out the other window. The moon was waxen. Vague jagged landscape and blurred rock formations rushed past in near total darkness. The wagon was picking up speed, hurtling recklessly now, the shuddering carriage violently jarred by the broken trail. It hit a big rock and rose off its wheels, slamming down on its suspension so hard it tossed him and the woman to and fro. She screamed again and held onto the leather hand straps for dear life. The bounty hunter leaned up against the window, pistols at ready and looked out, thinking he caught glimpses of big, bounding black forms keeping pace with the speeding stagecoach.

The loud, dull report of a shotgun blast sounded from the roof.

Then another.

Something hit the other side of the stagecoach like a boulder, knocking the wagon into a veering fishtail.

The old man released a horrible high-pitched scream of agony as his body was dragged off the roof seat and smashed against the door in a blur of cloth and red flesh with a bone-snapping *thud bang crack*.

The hooker saw the driver torn from the carriage and was screaming hysterically now. Whistler had to slap her silly to shut her up as he crawled across the seat to look out the other window. He fired two shots blind into the blackness, hopefully at least wounding a few of the things.

With a terrible crash, something landed on the roof so heavy it cracked the wooden ceiling.

The cowboy rolled onto his back, fanned and fired six times with his pistol up into the roof and blew the unseen monster on top of it off. He heard the beast land with a furry *thump* on the trail behind them with snarls of spitting fury.

Whistler still couldn't see anything, just hear it.

Keeping a pistol clenched in each gloved fist, the bounty hunter huddled with the cowering prostitute in the center of the madly charging stagecoach, listening to the deafening symphony of chaos outside the near total darkness of the hell-for-leather ride. The tambourine of the harnesses. The frightened whinnying. The din of galloping hooves just outside the cramped interior of the carriage. The crack of the whip sounded over that, then the report of the shotgun and in the muzzle flare, the flash briefly illuminated the hulking, hard charging beasts flanking the wagon. The stagecoach barreled on through the night, suspension jouncing on the rocks and stones of the broken trail. The small compartment pitched and yawed, throwing Whistler against the door. Out the open window, he saw the ghostly black shapes appear and disappear, the sound of their paws pounding the ground below the thunder of the horses. Whatever these beasts were they were big and incredibly fast.

They weren't outrunning them, that's for sure.

A giant claw on a furry black paw struck the door of the stage and dragged down, cutting through the wood.

"Get down!" Whistler roared to the shrieking hooker.

Something landed on the side of the rig, giant and hairy and malodorous. Its great weight heaved the carriage sideways, nearly tipping it as it came up on one wheel. Leaping up, he aimed his Scofield out the open window frame and fired twice point blank into the hulking form. The darkness was total but in the split-second flash of fire from his barrel he saw the great globular red eyes and the pink lapping tongue and long extended snout. The bullets hit their mark, and the thing was off the stage, tumbling in a cloud of dust on the side of the trail receding to their rear.

A pack of the creatures was running alongside the out-of-control carriage, like wolves at the heel of a deer, trying to take it down. The horrific roaring, snorting and snarling ripped the air.

The woman screamed again.

The door on her side was torn off completely. A black chasm gaped through the shattered-wood opening. Her hair and clothes were swept by the whipping wind. She clung to the frame on the door for dear life. Something had her from behind.

Time stood still.

Whistler stared regretfully into the hooker's bulging eyes, seeing her fingers slip from their purchase on the wagon. He did her a kindness by shooting her once in the forehead as sinewy black furred paws snatched her out with claws the size of carving knives.

The wolves fell back as the rig careened around a treacherous curve.

Whistler risked it and stuck his head out the opening to look up at the driver's perch. It was empty. The wagon was driverless, the galloping team of horses ready to send it to a ditch at any moment. Those monsters were still out there.

The bounty hunter was alone on the speeding stage and his guns were empty.

His Winchester carbine repeater was in the luggage on the roof.

Swinging out the open-door frame, Whistler reached up, grabbed the roof rail and began to pull himself out of the carriage. Immediately he was blasted by the wind from the hurtling wagon. As he struggled to haul himself up into the empty driver's perch, he used boots as well as hands for purchase but was nearly tossed off to certain death by the heaving motion of the stage. The huge bounding black shapes were everywhere behind him in the wake of dust off the wheels, resembling giant elongated wolves. As the hunter shrugged himself up with his arms and elbows onto the slatted seats, something grabbed his leg. He felt like his limb had been hit by an axe and a searing wetness spread across his entire calf. Ignoring the pain, the cowboy got all the way up on the top of the stagecoach and began reaching for his suitcase lashed to the roof. He tore off the ropes and pushed away the hooker's satchel, knocking it off the wagon top where it bounced to the ground and flew open scattering lingerie and undies. Then with both hands, he located his own suitcase and pulled the lid of his leather case open quickly to draw out his long steel Winchester repeater rifle.

Now armed, the bounty hunter confidently used the roof rack as a turret to steady his aim, opening fire on the rampaging creatures attacking the stage.

"Eat lead, you ugly sumbitches!" he shouted as he squinted down the gunsight and pulled the trigger and cocked the lever again and again. Fire erupted out the barrel as spent shells flew every which way from the breech. The beasts were struck by his shots right and left and fell and rolled, but they got up again. He cocked and fired, cocked and fired, and they went down and got right up and before he even considered he was running out of bullets, he knew this was no good.

A bear-sized black shape leaped on top of the team of horses and went to work with front and rear claws. Two more black shapes jumped at their legs and hamstrung the animals with their talons, bringing all two tons of stallion down at the same time in a terrifying jumble of harness and horse flesh and hooves. Bones snapped and bridles twisted. The chains of the harness linking the team to the carriage got tied up in the falling horses and the wagon impacted the whole huge knot of dead animals. The stagecoach flipped fifteen feet up in the air and spun twice before it came crashing to earth in smithereens of shattering wood, rent steel, flying wagon wheels and chassis parts. John Whistler was tossed a good hundred feet like a limp rag doll. He landed with a hard thud on the rocks and heard something inside him break.

Can't pass out, he told himself.

The man crawled for his gun.

His fingers touched the cold steel, and everything went funny.

Something struck his neck, and Whistler was rolling, the world turning over and over then right side up again. The ground was sideways. He saw his decapitated body lying ten feet away from him in his good suit, neck stump cleanly cleaved as the last oxygenated blood to his brain kept his severed head conscious for a few remaining seconds. His trunk was dragged by dark paws into the inky blackness as a huge fanged red maw swallowed his head whole.

CHAPTER TWO

ALVAREZ WOKE TO A WHITE-HOT SUN SEARING THRough his eyelids.

He was flat on his back in the burning desert sand.

The flesh of his arm was being ripped away.

And then the thief was screaming as he blinked his crusted eyes open to see the rotted pink head of the stinking buzzard, its foul yellowed beak tugging at a flap of wet red flesh on his bicep. God, the pain! Panic and terror turned his guts to jelly. Out of pure reflex, he grabbed for the gun in his belt, yanking it out of the holster to jam the muzzle into the vulture's black-feathered chest, pulling the trigger again and again.

Click click click.

Empty.

Shit!

It was coming back to him now how he used up all his bullets the night before and the horror he had used them on.

Right now he was being eaten alive by a carrion bird ripping a piece of his arm off while more vultures circled overhead. Adrenaline kicked in. Flipping the big Colt Navy pistol in his hand to grip it by the barrel, he wielded the wooden butt like a club, bringing it down again and again on the buzzard's fetid skull, beating its brains out. The vulture flapped its wings, blowing its stench, and screeched and cawed against the blows. "I am not dead yet, you stinking bastard!" the bandit cried hoarsely. "So you don't get to eat me! I kill you first! I kill *you!*" Alvarez brutally pistol-whipped the vulture until he felt the mottled skull cave in. Soft wet matter splattered his hair. Then the disgusting bird was down on the ground, not moving except for the death twitch of its limpid talons. The man laughed in demented triumph. "Who's dead *now*, eh? What, nothing to say? Hahaha! That's right, because it is *you* that is *dead,* you filthy fucking scavenger! I, Alvarez, am alive!"

Not for long.

Sitting up took great effort, as did staggering to his feet, but the wounded man managed to stand up. He swayed, dizzy from loss of blood, blinking away white spots in front of his eyes from the sun he'd been staring into. When his vision partially cleared he saw that he was alone in a sweltering desolate expanse of the Durango desert stretching out in all directions as far as he could see.

The dead vulture lay at his feet.

Alvarez shuddered at the memory of it feeding on him.

His dangling right arm throbbed in raw, savage pain. To his horror, the awful wound from the night before was festering. Bite marks of huge teeth punctured his swollen bicep like rows of bullet holes from elbow to shoulder. Blood was caked and dried over huge raking bruises on the rent flesh. The arm bone felt broken by the clamp of those monstrous jaws. He tried to move his fingers but they were numb and not working.

Now all at once he remembered the monster that wounded him last night; horrific memories of fangs and fur flooded back. A half-remembered nightmare that was all too real.

Filled with dread, the man looked around him until he located the stagecoach outpost in the distance. It jutted like a broken tooth out of the arid terrain a half a mile away. The small structure sat silent and still. Nothing moved inside, and from what he recalled, nothing would. Flocks of vultures flew in and out of dark windows that resembled eye sockets of a skull. More ugly buzzards perched on the wooden roof or circled like black fangs in the sky, attracted by the death that lay within. A path of his footprints in the sand led from the outpost up to where he had fallen and the indentation of his own shape on the ground with the wide dark stain of dried blood buzzing with flies. The stagecoach junction was a tomb, and while the little building afforded the only shelter from the deadly heat, he would sooner die before returning there.

But Alvarez knew he better find a doctor before gangrene set in.

It wasn't going to be easy.

The wounded man was in the middle of nowhere, engulfed by pitiless badlands vast and empty that seemingly went on forever. The sun was a searing oven, roasting him from on high.

What was he going to do? he wondered.

Better start walking.

Move those legs.

So he began taking clumsy steps, buckling under the punishing heat.

Touching the pocket of his trousers, Alvarez felt the bulge of the pouch; he still had his silver, what had gotten him into all this. Too bad he would not live to spend it because his wound was bad, so much blood lost, and there was nowhere to go for help.

But he kept walking.

And walking.

The day got hotter.

He grew closer to death with each unsteady step.

The wounded man would stagger over a hill in desperate hope he would spot some sign of civilization only to crest the rise to face more blasted empty terrain. In his delirium and despair, the thief was not sure how far he had walked before he saw the horses.

Two of them, in the distance; twin horses and riders melting like a mirage out of the watery waves of rising heat. He raised his hands above his head and flagged them down, praying that the *caballeros* and *hombres* astride them were not a hallucination.

Alvarez had fallen to his knees and wept in relief when the two Federales rode up, even though he had been running from them only yesterday. What a difference a day makes. Their tan button coats and caps blotted the sun as they sat in their saddles, light glinting off their brass buttons and the cartridges in their bullet belts. "I surrender, *señors*, please, take me in," the thief begged, and the obliging *policia federal* took him into custody directly.

The prisoner Alvarez sat at the table.

The rusty iron manacles bit his ankles.

The fat Federale sat across from him. The thin unshaven one leaned against the wall. They were inside a squat single-story outpost nestled in the foothills, a few miles from where he had been picked up. The police station, if it could be called that, was a hovel. Brick walls, dirt floors. A rifle rack in the corner. Two cots against the left wall. Empty whisky bottles. In the next room, he could see the bars of a cell. The air was close and stank of sweaty body odor.

And gangrene.

His arm wound had been washed and bound with a dirty cloth, but was infected. He could already smell the onset of necrosis. "I need a doctor," Alvarez groaned through teeth grit in pain.

"We said we will get you one," said the cop behind him. "After you talk."

They had found the silver when they searched him. The pouch sat on the table, out of his reach, and there was no point in lying to these men.

"My name is Pedro Alvarez," the prisoner began. "And I will tell you what you want to know." You bet you will, said the grim expressions on his captors' faces. One way or the other.

The fat one pushed a worn wanted poster showing a trio of *Americanos* under his nose. "Do you ride with these men?" the thin one barked. Alvarez stared dumbly at the hard faces of the three bad men in the crude sketches, but the letters on the crumpled paper meant nothing to him.

"Look at them!"

"He asked you a question, shit for brains!" The thief got punched in the back of the head by the cop against the wall.

"I can't read." Alvarez lowered his eyes in shame.

"Their names are Tucker, Bodie and Fix. *Hombres muy peligrosos.* Gringo gunmen down here who have done many robberies, killed many people with their fast *pistolas.* Do you ride with them?"

"No, *señors,* I do not know these men. I swear I have never seen them."

"You have not heard of the reward?"

"What reward?"

"You have never ridden with these gunfighters?"

"I do not know them!"

The fat officer punched the table with a beefy fist. "Then where did you get the silver? We know you stole it!"

"I am a thief. I robbed the money, as you said. It was a paymaster in Sinaloa but I did not kill him, *señors,* just hit him on the head a little bit, enough to drop him. This I swear to you on the grave of my mother. For the last three days I have been on the run. My plan was to catch the stagecoach at the Aqua Verde junction and escape to Mexico City, but the stage it never came. Last night, we had all of us been waiting there for hours at the junction when the trouble started."

"*Who* was waiting?"

"There were five of us. Two *vaqueros*, the man who sold the tickets and a fancy woman and her little girl. They steered clear of me, *señors*, because of my stench for not having bathed in days, and that was fine with me. I did not want to be noticed, you see. My brain was worried the Federales would catch up to me any minute, and if I did not get on that stage and get to Mexico City then I was a dead man." The prisoner laughed ironically. "Just a few hours ago, I thought getting arrested was the worst thing that could happen to me, but I was wrong. Now here I am, you caught me, and I am relieved because what I met up with last night was worse than anything the law could do to me."

"Don't bet on it."

"Put me in jail and throw away the key, *señors,* it would better than what attacked us. Here I am safe."

"Go on. Finish your story."

"The stagecoach did not come. Something else did."

"Is that what happened to your arm?"

Alvarez winced, clutching the gruesome bandaged wound in his bicep. "I need a doctor."

"That depends on your story."

"May I have a cigarette at least?"

One of the *policia* pushed over his fixings and matchbox. The thief spat on a piece of rolling paper, added a pinch of shag tobacco, closed it, licked it and put it to his lips. He struck a match and sucked smoke, coughing. "Maybe two hours passed. We looked out the window for any sign of the stagecoach. We would have surely seen its approach for the moon was full and very bright. You could look out and see the whole desert for many miles. But there was no dust on the horizon. And it was so quiet, *señors*, no desert sounds, no *insectos*, not even wind. No sweet music of the night. *Niente.* That is how I knew, how we all knew, something was very wrong. I admit I was very scared, *señors.*" His eyes widened in horror. "We heard them before we saw them. Howls, many howls, like wolves but not wolves. From everywhere."

The Federales exchanged dubious glances.

"It was an unholy sound that filled our hearts with fear. One of the *vaqueros* saw the first one through the window and when we rushed over there were many more, circling. Big, black shapes. Hairy. The ticket man took his rifle and fired into the things, shot many times, cocking his Winchester again and again but the bullets did not kill them and did not scare them off. So we locked the door and bolted the window shutters. That was when we heard the horses in the corral being killed. These were big horses, *señors,* but you should have heard their cries of pain and terror and the *repungante* sounds of meat being ripped from their bones and savagely devoured. *¡Qué horror!* What kind of animal is powerful enough to kill a full-grown horse and tear it to pieces, I ask you?"

"They were coyotes, you ignorant peasant!" The fat Federale glared in disgust at the bandit. "*Mira!* Have you never seen a coyote before?"

Alvarez shook his head vigorously, like a wet dog drying itself. "No, no, no. These things were big and fast, *muy grande* like coyotes but larger than men and their *teeth, señors,* such huge fangs! We pushed the stove and table against the door and windows but *los bestias* smashed and tore at the building with such force we felt the whole place shake. The little girl, she was screaming and her mother held her, but her mother she was hysterical too. I saw one *vaquero* get his head ripped off as a shutter caved in and a huge paw broke through the wood and those claws peeled the man's face from his skull like a banana and there was blood everywhere. The other *caballero* pissed himself when he saw his friend die in this way. You can bet I had my gun out by now and *bang,* I shot one of the claws off the monster and then I was at the window and fired right into its face, *bang bang bang . . .*"

Alvarez's eyes suddenly went glassy and unfocused. "I saw its *face.* It was not wolf and not man. It had jaws like a wolf and ears and fur like *el lobo* but the eyes, *señors,* its *ojos* were those of an *hombre. Sus ojos eran come rojos carbones.* I shot it in the face five times, not thinking I was wasting my bullets because there were so many *bestias.* The shots blew pieces off the monster's head, putting a hole in its skull and I saw the bloody brain." The thief's voice fell to a whisper. "And it grinned at me. A mocking grin, ear to ear. The bullets did not hurt it, *señors,* and in the ten seconds this happened, I saw its face grow back."

The fat Federale rolled his eyes and groaned as he listened but his partner was riveted, hanging on the bandit's every word. "What did you *do*?" He asked breathlessly like a small child. "What happened next?"

The storyteller went on with his tale, emboldened by the attention. "The shutters were being broken to pieces by the blows of the creatures. And their claws sheared through the wood. The ticket man was reloading his repeater when one of the beasts stuck its snout through the window and took the man's arm in its jaws and with one bite snapped it clean off. *Snap!* It *ate* the arm! So much screaming, so much blood. I was out of bullets and was going for the fallen *vaquero's* gun belt to get ammo to reload but at the same time keep my head down and duck the bullets his friend was shooting at the monsters, and that's when the damn kerosene lamp fell and the place caught fire. We had no choice but to flee."

Alvarez began to weep, recalling the horror that followed. "The rest happened very fast. As soon as we were out the door, one of the monsters grabbed the little girl right from her mother's arms in his teeth and swallowed the child in a single gulp. Then *su pobre madre* had her head ripped off. Another monster tore her headless body in half like a rag doll with meat inside. Everywhere, it was fur and claws and blood and arms and legs flying and guts all over the ground. I just ran into the darkness, *rápido como mis pies se iría*, to get away. Something bit my arm, crushed down on it like a bear trap right to the bone so I shot my last bullet into the red mouth and the jaws released me. I fled into the desert and heard the others' dying screams behind me and . . . this is all I remember, *señors*. When I awoke I was lying in the desert. And later you found me."

There was a clap. Then another. The Federale behind him was clapping his hands slowly and deliberately. "That's quite a story." The thin man nodded at his partner, impressed.

"Wolfmen." The fat one fingered one of his chins. "That explains everything."

"Yes, yes! *Gracias a Dios* you believe me!"

The cop leaned forward across the table, gaze dripping with contempt. "We did not say we believe you. In fact, we think you are a lying thieving piece of shit trying to bullshit us to save your sorry ass. Do you take us for fools?"

"Do you think we are assholes?"

"I think he's calling us *culos*."

"Insulting an officer is a crime. *Muy malo*. We can lock you up for a very long time. A very, very long time."

Alvarez did not like the way the obese cop was fingering the bag of silver. Or the knowing looks being exchanged between both the dirty *policia federal*. The fat, lazy Federale took a swig of whisky from the bottle. "Maybe I should ride over to the stagecoach junction and see if this *hombre*'s story checks out." He scratched his stomach. "There must be bodies all over the place, *si*?"

"If the vultures haven't eaten them," the thief said, worried no evidence might remain.

The thin one yawned, bored. "We'll go in the morning. My ass hurts and I want to take a nap. Then we'll get drunk and play cards."

"But *señors*, please! *Mi brazo!*" Alvarez pleaded, the throbbing agony of his mangled arm getting worse. Stabbing pain traveled through his shoulders and chest, like a hideous infection spreading through his bloodstream. *"Dijiste que me recibiría un medico."*

The thin Federale clicked his teeth. "Tsk. Tsk. *Si*, that bite is very bad. It already looks badly infected. I smell the gangrene." He sniffed like a rat. "You don't want *el doctor*, amigo. He will just take the arm. Cut it off."

"I need a doctor. We had a deal."

"You are a hard *hombre*, a *bandito*, tough it up!" The Federales laughed at each other, gold teeth glinting, and the thief understood there would be no doctor and he would die in jail. The *policia federal* meant to keep the silver and when he died from gangrene tomorrow or the next day they would bury his corpse in a shallow grave where the body would never be found. This was Mexico and that was how things were done.

"Fuck your mothers."

"Lock him up."

The thief was grabbed by the collar. The thin cop hauled him into the next room, a small chamber with two jail cells side by side. There were two occupants. An old sleeping drunk under a weathered brown sombrero and orange poncho was curled on the cot in the far cell. A filthy, muscle-bound laborer stood in the closer pen. The cop pulled out his keys and unlocked that cell, shoving Alvarez inside.

When he hit the floor, the shooting pain in his arm nearly caused him to pass out. When the thief looked up, his cellmate was giving him the stink eye. Alvarez was too wounded to resist as he felt the rough hands rummage through his pockets, stealing his last few pesos.

Alvarez was born poor and knew he would die in a pauper's grave.

❰

The *borracho* stirs in his cell.

The drunk old man is eighty-five, dressed in rags, sombrero resting over his face on the hard cot that hurts his brittle bones. But it is not the *clang* of the next cell door slamming shut that awakens him, although he is a light sleeper.

He knows by his smell the new prisoner is one of *them*.

The Men Who Walk Like Wolves.

The bum has met them before, long ago, in a life spent in the shitholes of Durango. While the old man's eyes aren't good and his hearing is failing, his nose works just fine and the distantly remembered stench comes back to him instantly. Once smelled, the odor of the werewolf is never forgotten.

He tilts the sombrero back from his eyes and studies the newcomer.

The wretch lies on the stained cement floor where the Federale who now locks the cell has brutally pushed him. His wound, a savage raking bite on his arm, festers yellow pus through the bandage the *policia* have carelessly applied. That explains it. The unfortunate has suffered the bite of the werewolf, and already the curse is in his bloodstream. Hence the smell, the acrid angry tang of bad blood, in the aged drunk's nostrils.

The attack must have happened last night, the *borracho* reckons, for the moon was full then as it will be again this evening. Casting a glance through his cell window, the old man sees the lowering sun in the sky. He knows in scant hours when the moon has risen the cell bars will no more hold the werewolf than tissue paper.

It will eat every human being in the jail.

After ripping them limb from limb.

Except the *borracho*.

No, it will not touch him.

For he has protection.

Even now, he feels its protuberance inside his worn boot beneath his foot, the obstruction pressing against the sweaty flesh of the arch. He always keeps it while traveling in these parts as a precaution. Nobody, not even the Federales who have him in custody, ever search his boots.

Few men trapped with a werewolf would see that as an opportunity, the old man muses. But if his eighty-five years have taught him anything, it is that any situation can be turned to a man's advantage and in every problem there is an opportunity.

One must just have patience.

So the drunk bides his time and sits and watches the poor soul in the cell adjacent, waiting for nightfall. Then, he knows, everything will happen quickly. The hours pass slowly.

The *borracho* has his plan all figured out.

Those *hijo de puta* Federales have kept him locked up behind bars for the past month, intending to let him rot and die here. They make no secret of it; the corrupt *policia* laugh when they tell him he will die in jail many times over recent days, tossing him table scraps to eat and not changing his overflowing slop bucket even once. Just because he had been drunk and taken a clumsy swing at one of them. The *borracho* had been riding through the area minding his own business when the bastards had accosted him and asked if he had money. Had he admitted he did, the old man knew those *cabronas* would have stolen it. When he said he had none, they arrested him for vagrancy. That's when he took the swing. An old man deserves respect. These filthy crooks in their unwashed uniforms are nothing more than pigs, but he is their prisoner. Until right this very moment, the *borracho* had resigned himself to die in this tiny, stinking cell.

Now he has hope.

In the other cage, the laborer who robbed the new prisoner stands by the bars counting a few paltry coins in his hand. The thief is smirking but the old man knows when the moon rises he will lose that smirk and those coins will be on the eyes of his corpse, if his eyes remain in his skull at all.

The last red glimmer of twilight fades on the windowsill.

The drunk stares without blinking through the bars into the next-door cell. The two men inside are now dim shadows in the bluish glow of moonlight. His eyes are not very good anyway, so he hears it first.

A choked cry of pain and surprise.

The figure of the wounded prisoner suddenly goes stiff, and then suffers a body spasm.

More sounds.

A sickening *snap* of bone.

A moist rending of flesh.

"What's wrong with you?" shouts the other convict, his darkened figure leaping to his feet to back away in alarm from the cellmate beginning to thrash spasmodically and froth at the mouth.

"Help, oh God help me!" The afflicted prisoner shrieks in agonized, awful high-pitched cries. Terrible noises follow . . . bones popping, skin tearing, rapid panting, the bristly sound of thick hair pushing through pores. Pale moonlight casts the seizuring convict's shadow across the floor and the shape begins to distort and distend, the arms and legs twisting and elongating in black exaggerated silhouettes.

In the next cell, the *borracho* has seen it all before. So he just watches. And makes himself ready.

"Help me oh God Madre Dios!"

"Shut the hell up in there!" booms the voice of one of the Federales in the other room.

"Hey, something's wrong with him!" yells the now genuinely frightened cellmate. "Get in here!"

"I said shut up!"

The jail is a deafening cacophony of unnatural sounds; scratching, pounding, flaying, splintering, smashing and splattering. In the lightless gloom, the shadowy figure of the new prisoner is changing, losing all human form, transfiguring in violently grotesque stages of anatomical distortion; becoming something *other*. To the old man's failing vision, this is all half-seen in shadow; quick glimpses of wiry fur and stretching flesh as the wildly flailing figure falls in and out of a thin slash of moonlight. Leg bones *crack* and reshape into haunches. The man's chest buckles inward with a sound like breaking chicken bones to become long and tapered. Talons punch out his fingertips like blunt knives through canvas. By now, the other convict is in a total panic, pressing against the bars, screaming to the *policia federal* to release him from the cell and the thing he is trapped with. "Get me out of here! You hear me?"

In the dark shadows behind him, the pitiful wretch suffers through the last of his tortured transformation. His voice changes, becoming guttural, hoarse and animalistic. *"Oh God Oh God it hurts it hurts it Oh GGGGGGGGGOO-OOOOOOGGGG-GGHHHHHHHH!!!"* The words slur into the growling roar of a beast.

A bushy tail flicks into the moonlight.

Frothing saliva foams over jagged white canine fangs, impossibly huge, bursting through gums.

The cell is small.

There is nowhere to run.

A new bad smell arises as the cellmate shits his pants, cowering in the corner as the abomination in the cage with him grows enormous, expanding to fill the cramped space as it towers against the ceiling. The silhouette of the furry chest becomes concave and narrow as a dog rib cage in a *crick-a-crack* of a spinal cord regenerating. The skull beneath the skin of the half-human face discombobulates as jawbones dislocate and break, an extended feral wolf-like snout punching out like a clenched fist. Hunched against the roof, the monster stands eight feet tall.

The werewolf is fully born and it wants meat.

The creature falls on the other man in the cell and tears his head and half his shoulder off the torso in a grisly wet splurge of chomped flesh with a whiplash *crack* of severed spine. It hungrily swallows the mouthful in one gulping bite.

This only whets its appetite.

The old man holds his sombrero in front of his face to shield himself from the tornado of gore and shorn flesh that explodes through the bars as the wolfman rips the convict's carcass apart in its huge talons and teeth, chewing and swallowing, reveling with feral abandon in the bloodthirsty carnage. Gallons of blood blast over the ceiling and gush down the iron bars of the abattoir of a cell like shiny black paint, splashing the sombrero but the only thing the old man feels is regret that his beloved hat is ruined for it has been with him for as long as he can remember.

All is going to plan.

It takes those damn fool Federales long enough to get there.

But now they stand in the doorway, eyes like saucers, frozen in place as they witness the monster filling the cage to bursting. The wolfman is covered with shags of flesh and ropes of eviscerated intestine, a severed half-chewed human arm in its gory mouth.

The old man does not move a muscle, even though the werewolf is mere feet from him. It has not seen or smelled him yet.

It just noticed the *policia*.

Wait for it, he tells himself over and over.

One of the ignorant cops fumbles his pistola out of its holster and opens fire on the creature behind the bars, the bullets hammering it back, as the other officer runs to the office and quickly returns with a bolt action rifle that he has to load and fire one big round at a time as if any of those bullets do any good.

They simply punch holes through the monster's chest that quickly heal.

And piss it off.

Inflamed by the sting of the bullets and hungry for more flesh, the werewolf leaps at the bars and the men jump back, bathed in sweat as they clumsily reload. The monster's slavering jaws stretch impossibly wide and it emits a petrifying roar of frustration and fury. Clenching the cage in its talons, the creature yanks and jerks with all its incredible strength, trying to pry the cell door loose.

Those bars will not hold. The old man smiles to himself.

You Federales should have run while you had the chance.

Werewolves are above your pay grade.

But no, the dumb cops feel foolishly secure with more bullets in their guns and they blast the monster again and again through the bars. The gunshots are ear-splitting in the enclosed space, along with the roars of the wolfman. Muzzle flashes ignite the total darkness of the room like lightning bolts, revealing the gigantic, hairy, haunched, fanged creature in strobing staccato flashes. The smoke-thick air stinks of gunpowder, cordite, coppery blood and human bile and excrement. The *borracho* covers his nose as he huddles in his cell, watching the show. The bullets take chunks of hair and skin off the beast in the cage, so out of its mind with fury its psychotic eyes bulge in mad swirls of red as it uses the talons of its massive paws wrapped around the bars to tug them free of the cement foundations.

Then the bullets stop.

The cops' guns are empty.

It is too late to run but they try anyway.

They get maybe three feet.

The werewolf tears the cell door off the frame and pounces out, bringing both men down with two sledgehammer paws into a pool of darkness in the corner of the corridor. There are sounds of screaming and arms and legs being torn out of their sockets and skulls being crushed and rib cages splintered and bitten into amidst all the growling, slobbering and chomping. It is a hard way for the men to die, but the *borracho* has no pity for them.

The old timer guesses the creature will finish this meal in less than a minute and be looking for seconds.

It will see him then in the cell.

And break through the bars to get him.

This is the plan.

It is time.

The old man pulls off his right boot and dumps its contents out, which *clank* on the darkened floor.

The object glints in a ray of moonbeam.

A two-shot Derringer pistol.

Picking the gun up, the *borracho* snaps the twin barrels open to expose the two sterling silver bullets he has loaded there. *Clicking* the chambers shut, the old man squeezes into the corner of the cot, waiting for the monster to break into his cell.

The sounds of the feast cease. The revolting wet *slurping* of the wolfman lapping up the last morsels in the gloom of the jail.

The old man whistles.

A sudden angry growl of surprise and the monster rears in the darkness, a towering shape blacker than the other shadows. The silhouette of the huge canine head rotates, nostrils sniffing.

He whistles again, letting the wolfman know he is there. The old man understands the smell of booze on him has disguised his smell. But now the monster is alerted to his presence. Its red eyes glow like coals and fix on the *borracho* in the cell, noticing him for the first time.

With a deafening throaty roar, the creature launches itself at the old man's jail door with both talons, grasping and wrenching on the bars in berserker rage, tail swishing. It uses its ferocious razor-rowed teeth to try to bite through the iron rods, so mad and unquenchable is its appetite.

"Come and get me!" the chuckling old man taunts, egging the beast on.

It is halfway through the cage.

Readying himself, knowing he will only have two shots and mere seconds to place them, the old man raises the Derringer and settles the notches of the short muzzle on the broad furry chest of the werewolf ripping out the bars of his cell.

Patience.

Paciencia.

The wild-eyed monster pulls at the bars, prying them loose, the metal buckling against the crumbling cement of the fixture.

Esperar.

Wait.

CRRR-RRAAANK! Three iron rods break free of the ceiling as the wolfman tears the cell door loose and shoulders through the gap like a hairy battering ram, bending the bars as it squeezes through, claws swiping a foot from the face of the old man with the pointed gun. Its snapping bear-trap jaws clamp shut so close the *borracho* feels the spray of its foul spit on his face and smells the hot stench of its gullet. Then there is the sound of tortured metal as the whole cell door collapses inward and the werewolf is inside the cage.

Now.

Ahora!

The old man fires his Derringer twice, pulling both little triggers, putting two silver bullets clean through the werewolf's heart before it gets another step.

The wolfman drops in its tracks, instantly dead.

As the lifeless body hits the floor, there is a flurry of movement as immediately the monster's physiognomy twists and reforms back into the crumpled figure of a dead naked human being on the ground.

The old man rises at last.

Everyone in the jail is dead but him.

His cell door is open, broken off the hinges.

He walks through it a free man.

The luck of the drunk. Tonight, he vows to say a prayer to the moon, the patron saint of werewolves, for the good fortune she bestowed on him.

Stopping just long enough to do a few things before his departure, the old man is soon on his way. He rummages through the pockets of the Federales' remains and takes their wallets. Selecting two fresh rifles and two pistols from the gun rack in the office, he takes enough ammo to last him awhile. Two bottles of whisky are now his. The last thing the *borracho* takes from the police station is the pouch of silver on the table that he stuffs in his pocket with the bullets. Then, selecting the strongest horse from the corral outside, he saddles up and rides west.

CHAPTER THREE

THE ONE CALLED TUCKER LEANED BACK IN THE CHAIR, put his dusty boots up, spurs clinking, and squinted out at the harsh Durango desert that lay beyond the porch of the rundown cantina. One big empty. The sun was just rising, already blinding, and he dipped his hat brim to shadow his face. It was going to be another hot damn day. The man was tall and lean, the shag of beard bare by the scar on his jaw but thick across the rest of his sunburned leathery face. He rolled a cigarette and lit it between thick fingers, with cauliflower knuckles broken several times on others' faces, and sucked in the good hurt of the bad tobacco. His Colts hung heavy in his holsters. Flies buzzed in the air.

He didn't like the way the peasant was staring at him.

The Mexican had been there for an hour standing across the street, sizing him up. Usually these villagers kept their distance, keeping their eyes and heads down, avoiding trouble, but this little brown man had been looking at him with interest for a while now. Maybe they didn't get too many gunfighters around here, the bunghole of the earth.

Slapping an annoying fly on his cheek stubble, the gunfighter wiped the crushed insect off his palm on the wooden post, settling back in his chair with a creak of leather as he shifted his boots.

The dismal outpost was nestled in the desert flats one hundred twenty miles from Villahidalgo for travelers passing through on the Santa Maria Del Oro trail. It wasn't much, just a cantina, feed store, barn and a ramshackle corral. Tucker had his horse tethered there along with those his compatriots rode. The gunfighter had been here a week, lying low with the other two, planning their next move. He wondered how the hell he'd ended up here. The only other human beings he'd seen were the occasional Mexican farmers who rode through to purchase supplies for the few poor scattered villages throughout the area. None of the peasants had given him so much as a passing glance.

Until this one.

The brown man stood across the street from the cowboy, watching him sitting on the porch smoking his cigarette.

And this way they killed a few more minutes.

It was just a harmless peasant, Tucker decided, who didn't appear to be armed, though he didn't know that for sure. Unwashed wretch was covered with filth, his face smeared with caked mud, grime and sweat. The cowboy wondered if these people bathed, and this one was the dirtiest he had ever seen. By habit, the shootist gauged the possible threat this stranger might pose to him on this barren morning and how he would handle it. The peasant was alone. Impoverished as he clearly was, he may have recognized Tucker from the wanted posters and thought he would try for the reward to feed his family. He had no rifle but could possibly have a pistol under his baggy clothes. Might be he had a knife or machete there instead. If the loiterer stepped within ten feet of him, Tucker would draw his gun. The man would be dead in the dirt before he drew down. The gunfighter was fast, very very fast. That was why he'd lived to age thirty-four.

The lazy minutes passed. Tucker finished his smoke, pitched it with a flick of his fingers, and crossed his hands over his tight stomach, fingers inches from his Colt Peacemakers in the holsters slung from his chaps. The peasant didn't move.

Squinting up the street, he saw Fix sauntering up the block in his suit and bowler hat, pistols at his sides. Thin as a rail, a black mustache on his face, beady eyes that didn't miss a thing, the other man gave a tiny nod of acknowledgment.

"Who's the sombrero?"

Tucker shrugged. "Been giving me the eyeball last hour."

Fix regarded the peasant with a squinty black bullet eye. Quicker than any man Tucker knew to size up a threat, he was the fastest to dispatch it. The other cowboy was small, didn't move much and was a man of few words, but he struck with the lethal speed of a scorpion. Fix took a chaw off a plug of tobacco and spat, squinting at the Mexican. "Looking for a handout?" he said.

"Mebbe."

"Could be looking to get hisself the reward on us."

"Mebbe."

"Where the hell's Bodie?"

"Sleepin' it off."

"Right."

"Mexican's still there."

"Yup."

"We're flat broke. I got three dollar."

"Then you're holding all the money."

"The hell is Bodie?"

A sound of something heavy falling, a vulgar curse and muttered grumbling answered his question. There was more banging, more cursing. Tucker and Fix turned their heads to see the third of their number, Bodie, stumbling around the side of the cantina. The Swede was a massive man, six foot five and thick as a buck and rail fence. His face was a square boulder set with sleepy, slow eyes and laugh lines around a mouth quick to smile. A lock of blond, uncombed hair fell along his face. With a broad, cracked grin, Bodie leaned against the wall beside Tucker's chair. He tightened his cartridge belt around his waist, from which swung twin Remington Army revolvers. "Boys, my head's comin' apart. Right shorely it is."

"Hair that bit ya." Fix tossed Bodie a silver flask. Bodie took a swig.

"We need money, boys," Tucker said, looking out at the sun lifting just above the horizon. He hated being broke, and this had been a bad spell. The gunfighter needed to make some cash quick or starve and he'd been considering their options. Most promising was a small cattle drive they'd ridden past in Juarez. Two days' ride and Tucker, Fix and Bodie could catch up with the four wranglers, mostly kids, who wouldn't stand in the way long of gunmen the ilk of he and his partners. They could either tie the wranglers up or shoot them, then haul the stolen cattle down to one of the many ranches near Mexico City and sell them for five bucks a head. It wouldn't be the first time they'd resorted to thieving. He didn't like it, but a man had to make a buck.

"Scalps is selling for a good price." Fix used his Bowie knife blade to clean some dirt from under a fingernail.

"We don't do that," Tucker whispered.

"Maybe we should start."

"I don't trade in no hair." Bodie shook his head in disgust.

"Me neither."

"Well we better figure our situation out and get a plan, or we're going to be eating sombrero over yonder."

"Plan is saddle up. Time to move. Can't stay around here." Tucker grunted.

"Thought we were going to lie low until them Federales moved on."

"They may have already done."

"We don't know that."

"Point is, we just can't sit around this hole rottin' away forever."

"Bodie's right. We're getting lead in our ass. Man's gotta keep moving." They were men of action and do or die they needed to saddle up.

"That peasant's gettin' on muh nerves. What's he doin', just standing there?"

The three big tough gunslingers lounged on the porch of the cantina and looked at the Mexican.

He was coming across the street toward them.

Finally, they would learn what he was after.

As he came in their direction, the peasant doffed his sombrero, kowtowed and submissive as a dog who'd been beat too much. He stopped at the edge of the porch, where the gunmen fingered their triggers. "Please, *señors*, may I speak to you?"

Tucker fired up another rolled cigarette and targeted the stranger with a glowering stare through the fire of the match. "What do you want?"

The humble Mexican peasant stood before them, sunburnt head bowed, holding his straw hat contritely. He was in his late teens with soft features, baggy clothes and a quiet voice. "We are poor, we have no money to pay," he said. "They have killed our women and children. This is not the worst of it, *señors*. They have taken over the church. In our village, our church was Santa Tomas, but now the people call it Santa Sangre. Saint Blood. Those who have come, they drink our blood, eat our flesh, they are men that walk like wolves. Will you help us, please?"

The gunfighter Tucker looked at the other two gunslingers, spat in the dust and spun the cylinder of his revolver. "What's in it for us?"

"Silver."

"Thought you said you didn't have no money."

"It is the silver in the church. Plates. Statues. A fortune, *señor*."

"It belongs to the church."

"The church of Santa Sangre now belongs to them, *señor*."

"So we kill them for you, we take the silver, that the deal?"

"You will need the silver. You will need it to kill them, *señor*. You must melt it down into bullets that you shoot through their hearts. It is the only way to destroy the werewolf. What silver is left after you kill them, you may keep."

"How many?"

"Many."

"We'll think about it."

"But you must leave now. Tonight is the full moon."

Tucker studied his spurs, then looked laconically sideways at his comrades.

Bodie shrugged.

Fix clicked his teeth, which meant fine.

None of the three gunfighters bought the Mexican's story.

Except the part that there was a church and it had silver.

If it was there, it was there for the taking.

Tucker rose to his feet and grinned down at the peasant. "Hell, we got nothing better to do today."

Without further discussion, the shootists ambled over to the corral for their horses. The peasant fetched his own from behind the barn. They all swung into their saddles.

The four riders rode out.

The length of fabric tightly tied around her upper torso, flattening her large breasts, made her bosom itch beneath the canvas shirt. The cloth was coming loose in the up and down motion from the horse. She wished she'd tightened it back by the cantina, worried her bind would come off and concealed tits bounce, giving her away. The girl felt dirty and squalid and yearned for a bath, but the filthier she was the better.

Before riding into the outpost, she smeared mud and dirt all over her face to help disguise the womanly contours of her features, and the grit was now caked with crud, but so be it. The three gunfighters did not know she was a girl. She wanted to keep it that way. These hard men must not learn her sex if she was to keep her virtue.

Her name was Pilar.

The four riders galloped across the arid Durango desert plain. They slowed the horses every few miles, then spurred them on again, pacing their animals against the brutal heat beginning to bear down. They'd need to make time now, because the horses would be exhausted and slower by the time noon hit, the sun a kiln overhead, and their progress would be impeded. It would take hours to prepare for the battle ahead and they had to reach the village by noon to be ready by nightfall.

The gunfighters' horses were big and hers was small. It was a simple, scrawny mustang from the humble stables in her poor town, the best they had. Her small ankles kept rubbing against the ribs sticking out of her pony. The animal had not been properly broken and kept tossing its head against the bit in its mouth, but she held her reins firm in her small soft fists and maintained control of the mount. It must not throw her and run off. Her life and that of her entire village depended on Pilar getting these men there and she must not fail. She had never known such a burden or felt so alone. Again and again, as the girl rode, she prayed quietly to herself that she and her warriors would arrive in time and in one piece. God must not abandon her in their time of need.

The sound of sixteen hooves thundered across the parched desert and scrub. Pilar kept her horse in the lead, following the tracks of the trail she made riding in a few hours ago. Her ears were good. Behind her back, she heard the men talking to one another, keeping their voices low but not low enough, likely figuring she did not understand them, but she did. The Tennessee missionary who had been their village's reverend had seen to that, teaching her how to read and speak English from childhood.

"The Mexican says it's a three-hour ride to Santa Sangre," the strong one was saying.

"It's mebbe mid-morning."

"You buy this Mexican's story?"

"Not a word."

"Except the silver part."

"And we're going to steal the whole damn thing."

What did she expect, wondered Pilar. They were men of the world, susceptible to greed, yet something in her trusted that they would do the right thing when the time came. To come face to face with the monsters would make anyone kill them. Have patience and fortitude, she reminded herself as the saddle slapped her sore thighs; these men could not be any worse that what had come to her village.

Her only worry was them discovering she was a girl and that they would rape her before they reached town. She was a virgin, and these were dangerous men who would take her virtue if they knew, because men such as these did as such men do. But right now, her secret was safe.

"Hey, Pablo. Ain't *sangre* the Mexican word for blood?" The tall, handsome one she had first observed was speaking to her.

"*Si*," she called back, lowering her voice to a manly timbre.

"Why the heck you go and name your church something like that?"

"The name of our church was changed to Santa Sangre because of the terrible thing that has happened there."

The same one she first laid eyes on in the town spoke roughly as he rode up beside her, leather chaps squeaking and spurs clinking as his knees clenched the saddle.

"Okay, Pancho. We want the whole damn story, no bullshit. What the hell is going on in your town?"

"The werewolves changed the name of our church. It is they who called it Santa Sangre, in honor of their God."

"Start from the beginning."

They all slowed their horses to a trot so the frothed, lathered animals could catch their breath and the men could hear. The sun now hung at nine o'clock, rising ever higher, burning like a white bullet hole in a slate sky. They had three hours to make Santa Sangre by noon.

On the long hot ride, the peasant told the gunmen her tale . . .

Remember, Pilar, remember it all.

Every detail of the horror.

These men must know so they can be ready.

Oh Pilar, last month seems like a lifetime ago.

So many friends gone.

The way they died.

The town a shell.

My home, hell on earth.

I don't want to remember, don't want to think back and weep because only women cry and that would give myself away, but tell the tale I must, so these fearsome men believe what they are up against.

That long first night, bracing the shutters of our windows closed with both hands to keep out the howling so loud it shakes the boards under my palms, coming from everywhere, everywhere . . .

The village was warm earlier that evening and everyone was on the streets as I ended the lesson and told the children to run home. The little ones are laughing. Small Pablo needs a bath. Tiny Maria is so pretty with the bow in her hair. They gather their books and get up to leave my class-room as I erase the chalkboard. The sky was red. I stepped out the door onto the dirt and smelled the dust and mesquite, straw and dung of the fine evening air. The smell of home. The road passes through the huts and corrals and my farmer neighbors in sombreros and ponchos ride by on burros and horses, their carts full of hay and sheep. I smile at my friends. The church bells ring, and I look up the hill to see the steeple of Santa Tomas watching over us.

I am almost home and listen to the coyotes yip in the desert, their familiar high-pitched, keening yelps echoing near and far, front and behind. We must bring the dogs in tonight. The coyotes stop their calling, as if frightened. It was then, one month ago today, when our town first heard the baying howls out in the mesas. How I remember the pale near full moon that hung in the skies, so huge, so white, the color of rotten milk. Out in the fields, I see two farmers my age, Manuel and Roja, tending their meager crops. They whirl at a terrible sound and look far out into the hills, eyes wide in fear. The howling was so loud it shook the ground, a cry like wolves, but bigger and much, much worse. Roja dropped his rake and rushed back to the village. Such commotion in the square. Everyone is rushing to their huts, tying off their horses, grabbing their wives and children, and hurrying inside their homes.

Yes, good, the three dangerous gunmen riding with me are listening closely now, leaning in their saddles to hear, eyes glinting with interest, and I have their attention.

Mama!

I flee home and as I run past the other huts I look through the open doors and windows being shuttered and bolted and see throughout the village the families huddled fearfully in their hearths. Over there Gabriel and Maria peer nervously out their window into the dark and empty square, and there, the frightened eyes of Jose duck down through the window of the next hut. The dogs in the town bark feverishly until the howls grow too loud and even the strongest dog cowers. When I reach my place I bolt the door and window and stay with Mama. In her eyes was a fear I'd never seen.

"Como?" I ask.

"*Antiguo unos*," she whispers. "*Hombres lobos*."

I had seen the pictures in the cave on the hill the ancient ones drew when the moon was young, telling the legend of the men who walked like wolves, but it was a children's tale, and I did not believe such foolishness, so reckless was I. They had returned. Maybe they had never left.

The door and windows we shut with heavy wood and iron bolts, but we could hear, oh could we hear. The roaring outside the town tightening around us like a noose. The plates shook in the kitchen. It sounded as terrible as if they were right outside, but they were still in the hills. At last I can stand sitting still no more and must know what is out there. Over my mother's pleas, I pry her hands from my dress and rush to the window, pulling back the bolt over the slot that my father had built just large enough to stick the snout of a gun through. I press my eye to the opening and first just see the darkness so dense all is shadow. Why does this nearly full moon, so large and awful, cast no light? I make out the bumps of the other huts. Big, rearing shapes in the stalls where the horses rise on their hind legs in terror, their eyes white in the gloom bulging with terror. The howls from the unseen ones hurt my ears through the door slot, but I can also hear the whinnying and pounding hoofs of the panicked horses pawing ground, and the squealing of the pigs and bleating of the sheep, although I cannot see their stalls. Yet the streets are empty, as my eye adjusts to the darkness. Our village huddled in fear. The moon hung like a great silver platter, more omnipresent than before. Out in the mesas, the howling persisted, trapping us.

The hours pass and men of the village have gathered their rifles and stand now outside their houses, protecting their wives and young from what is to come. We pray for it to be soon, we want it to be over. The men's eyes are like saucers as the night moves on. Each are within view of the others, and they make hand signals, pointing, patting their palms down; wait for it, do not move from where you stand is their meaning.

Still they did not come.

The monsters announced themselves in the hills but chose to remain concealed, staking their territory. The snarling was a bloody thunder that shook the ground to let us know they could take any of us anytime they wanted, conjuring awful pictures of what they looked like that were nothing compared to the horror of when finally we laid eyes on them.

But it was not to be that night.

We waited, sleeplessly, quivering in terror and the howls never stopped, never relented.

Remember, Pilar, the fear you knew then, it is in your voice now you tell your gunmen, and that is good, because they know you tell the truth. Look at their eyes now, in the saddles alongside you, exchanging glances with one another, disbelieving and believing and not sure what to believe.

Keep talking, the small one with the white-handled guns says.

I realize I have stopped speaking, the emotions too great and my throat choked with dust. But I have not cried, not yet. They must hear the whole tale. I continue my story and go on about that first terrible sleepless night, how we stood awake and counted the hours and the seconds with the men holding their guns and the women clutching their children until dawn broke, and by then we were tired and drained with fear and our nerves were raw. This was the werewolves' plan, do you see, señors? They were tiring us out, grinding us down, robbing us of rest before they descended for the kill, driving fear into us as a picador spears a bull to make him weak for the matador. The howling ended at sunrise, and with daylight somehow we knew we were safe. A bleached-out sun rose over our meek village. Some said they were gone. Some said they would be back.

Two farmers walked into the hills, herding their sheep. I was told they saw a trail of blood and scattered rags leading into the brush. My townsmen followed the blood trail fearfully, and what they encountered caused them to drop to their knees and cross themselves before they buckled over and vomited. They brought him back in a bag. The mutilated remains of Manuel torn limb from limb and eaten by something much more powerful than a coyote.

We knew it was no coyote, señors.

CHAPTER FOUR

IT WAS THE CRAZIEST DAMN YARN TUCKER EVER HEARD.
He'd have disbelieved every word if he hadn't heard it from the peasant's own lips. The simple Mexican's terror was real. It made the cowboy wonder what they were going up against. He wasn't exactly sure, but his gut was they were going to earn whatever money they were going to make.

The sun was now forty-five degrees above them, burning down mercilessly in the iron sky. They'd been on the trail for about an hour now and were feeling the heat of the day. Across the plain, the three gunfighters and the peasant kept at a brisk trot as the Mexican paused the story to sip from his canteen, shuddering at the harrowing memories. Tucker exchanged glances with Fix and Bodie and from the uneasy expressions of his cohorts saw they were just as unnerved by what they'd heard.

The little man decided the horse had had enough rest, dug his sandals into the flanks of his brown mustang and urged it into canter, and the other riders followed suit.

It was as if the devil were snapping at the peasant's heels as he rode hard for a town three hours somewhere ahead. Hooves pounded the parched rocks and pebbles of the trail, shrouding them in a cloak of dust that made the figures of the horses and riders tall silhouettes. All around them stretched unbroken desert until the far-off distant turquoise and purple ridges of the tan and dun Sola Rosa mountains.

Fifteen minutes later they spotted a gleaming blue thread in a chaparral-strewn arroyo south of them.

Tucker yelled ahead over the loud clop of the hooves at the hunched back of the hard-charging peasant. "There's a river yonder south! Let's water the horses!" He had to shout it three times at the top of his lungs before the brown man's startled, haunted face looked back over his shoulder. The Mexican nodded as he tugged on his reins and reared around his horse to ride back next to the slowing mounts of the others.

"Whoa. Whoa," Bodie said, patting the side of his stallion's sweat-soaked neck.

"Take a break," growled Fix, who never smiled.

"This was some bad idea," complained the Swede, wiping his sopping hair with his filthy Stetson. "It's crazy hot out here."

"Stop yer bitchin'. It ain't even noon. Then you'll see hot." Fix spat a loogie of tobacco juice.

"That's why we ride in the afternoon and evening and always done since we got south of the border," griped Bodie.

"Mexican wants to make his town by noon, and that's the deal we made and it's what we're gonna do. Suck it up," Tucker bossed. "Right now, let's wash these nags down before they keel."

Tucker rode out in the lead and they negotiated their way over the uneven ground until they came up a small incline leading past the cactus and boulders down into the draw. A creek trickled past over the gleaming dark damp stones.

Tucker hauled off his hat and hunkered down by the edge of the creek. He felt that dull ache in his leg from the bullet he took a year ago in Arizona. They pulled the slug out but the pain was getting worse, a little each month. How long was he going to be able to ride, he wondered, getting an uncomfortable intimation of his own mortality. Cupping both dirty weathered hands, he splashed some water on his face and enjoyed the refreshing, bracing chill of the fresh creek. The drops trickled down his chin and with one hand he spooned a few sipfuls into his parched lips. Then he dunked his canteen, turning the steel mouth toward the flow of the river, and watched the bubbles percolate up into the rapids. With a grunt, he stood and straightened.

Squinting, the big gunfighter peered to where Fix and Bodie stood chatting a few yards away by their horses that were tethered to the tree batting their noses against each other. Bodie had fired up a cigar and was blowing a cloud of acrid smoke. Just then, the Swede's colt's dangling member blasted a huge yellow jet of urine explosively onto the ground and splashed his owner's legs and boots, resulting in a burst of cussing and flailing from Bodie, who punished the horse by punching it square in the jaw with a clenched club fist. The cowboy hurt his hand more than the horse and yowled, shaking his fingers and dancing around hugging his fist. Fix thought this was funny, and buckled over convulsively in laughter, slapping his knee. Bodie tossed his piss-drenched cigar onto the ground and stomped it to pieces, stalking away, while Fix chortled even harder, until he began to cough and spit. Tucker wasn't laughing.

The Mexican was gone.

Tensing, Tucker saluted his hand over his brow to block the sun and scanned the area this side of the draw. No sign of the peasant. About to take a walk to start looking, he caught a sudden movement in the corner of his eye. The peasant rose from some drab green mesquite bushes, tying the rope belt around his britches. The small figure started walking back toward the arroyo, keeping his head down, and Tucker eyeballed the smooth, graceful movements he made. This was the prettiest man he'd ever seen, the gunfighter remarked to himself. That brown skin was soft and unblemished even for those people, the lips were soft and full, and the peasant's smell was sweet and appealing for a man even after at least a day's ride without bathing. The body odor of the peasant reminded him more of the Mexican whores he'd been with over the last few months. If Tucker didn't know better . . .

The Mexican jumped down the row of small boulders to the rubble near the draw and walked to his horse, untethering its hemp bridle and leading it to the creek, where the unkempt mustang ducked its big head and drank.

Tucker kept his eyes fixed on the peasant, watching the way the man tenderly stroked and kissed the horse with an almost feminine gentility to his movements.

Yes, if he didn't know better . . .

Damn.

"You believe this Mexican's story?" Fix whispered.

Tucker didn't notice that his partners had walked up beside him, grouping close and whispering out of earshot of their new saddle buddy.

"The Mexican's a fool, either ignorant or crazy," replied Bodie.

"A fool and his money are easily parted," Tucker stated flatly. Passing a flask of whisky, they took turns taking pulls and watching the peasant in rags sitting on a rock praying desperately to a cross on a string of beads in his hands. "And it's easy money, boys."

"Damn easy."

"I'll drink to that." Bodie chuckled and swigged the hooch.

"Go easy on that. It's got to last us," Fix scolded.

"I feel sorry for the sad sunufabitch." Bodie belched with the smell of corn.

Not that sorry, Tucker observed, seeing the opportunistic glint in his saddlemate's blue eyes. Himself, he was having his doubts about the rightness of robbing a sorry wretch like this Mexican. But he and his friends needed the money, and these were tough times. They had fallen hard, he ruminated, things having come to this.

A wave of self-doubt seemed to pass through all three men, who often thought the same thing at the same time. The gunfighters exchanged glances and shrugged it off. Time to act, not think.

By now it was late morning, and the riders had stopped to rest their horses in the shady mesquite ravine by the burbling creek long enough. Too easy to get lazy and dawdle, when there was work to be done. Tucker, Bodie and Fix wet down their animals one last time.

"We don't even know there *is* any silver," Fix said.

They looked at each other. It was true.

Tucker shook his head, pondering, his brain masticating over the situation like an itch he couldn't quite scratch. "That town has come up against something, that's for damn sure. That wretch is scared spitless, anybody can see that. I say he's telling us the truth, or least what he thinks is. Likely, it's just bandits. But bad ones."

"I got no problem killing bandits," said Fix. "But we're keeping the silver. Our regular rounds should do them vermin right nicely." To accentuate his point, the thin, spare gunfighter drew out his pearl-handled Colt, flipped open the cylinder with a flick of his wrist, checked his bullets, peered down the barrel, shook the gun closed with a metallic *whirr* and spun it backward on his finger with a blur of speed back into his holster.

"Then we keep all the silver." Bodie grinned. "Dumb peasants won't know the difference." He pulled his Winchester repeater out of his saddle holster and put it to his shoulder, eyeballing a distant target down the gunsight. His finger tightened on the trigger but he didn't fire, saving bullets.

The bad men drank to that. They swung back into their saddles.

Tucker stuck both boots in his stirrups and felt the beginning sting of saddle sores.

Across the arroyo the little Mexican peasant saw them mount up, giving them a nervous little wave as he tugged himself back up onto his own horse.

"Hy-Yahh!" Tucker yelled as he slapped his reins against his stallion's flanks. The other three riders charged after him up the ninety-degree arroyo grade, powerful hooves kicking down some chaparral and stones. Fix's horse slipped and regained traction and then they were all four up and over the incline and galloping off toward the trail. Catching the peasant's gaze, Tucker nudged his jaw for him to ride ahead and lead the way, and filled with purpose, the Mexican retraced the trail of his hoof prints that he had taken into town.

They rode across the Durango plain in the heat of the day. A second ridge of mountains appeared beyond the first, brown in the flat light and spackled with green. The washed-out sun had risen a few more degrees, and the day would get hotter yet before they reached their destination. And so the battery escort of hired gun killers flanked the hunched, determined brown man they accompanied. Everyone figured that their newly watered horses were refreshed enough to ride at full tilt for twenty minutes before they slowed again. The outfit was making good progress.

They all rode together up a small mountain trail of the first butte.

The humble peasant smiled with simple, pure faith at the three hard men riding along with him.

"You are good men, *señors*."

"You don't know nothing about us," Tucker said quietly.

"I do." The Mexican rode eagerly on ahead, out of earshot. "I do . . ."

The three bad men eyed him like coyotes.

"He don't know the half," uttered Fix.

"Like we aim to steal that silver, not waste it on no bullets," added Bodie humorlessly.

"That's for damn sure," Tucker said, half-convinced himself.

"Ignorant wretch is letting the wolf into the chicken coop and don't know no better." Fix spat tobacco juice onto a passing lizard and scattered it into the rocks.

Tucker considered the thin, skeletal gunfighter in the black suit and vest covered with dust. He'd ridden with Fix for three years and as long as he'd known him, the other gunfighter was the most pitiless man he had ever met. A good friend, who said what he meant, without question the fastest and deadliest shot of the bunch, but the man had no mercy towards people. John Fix had a fatalistic view of the human condition and his place in it. His tough-mindedness balanced off Bodie's impulsivity and Tucker's measured deliberateness. But Fix was a gunsel only, a man who dealt with things as they appeared in front of him, where he struck swiftly and without remorse. He lacked Tucker's own grasp of the big picture and habit of planning a few steps ahead, which was why Samuel Evander Tucker, late of Dodge City, was the group's unspoken but unchallenged leader. The three had rode together through the years simply because it seemed like the natural thing to do from the day they first met, never with any specific plan, and every day they seemed to make the decision anew to stick together. When they fought, when their guns came out, they were no longer three, but one, an invincible machine of flying lead, stinking gunpowder and blazing irons, and they killed and shot as one thing with six arms and legs and they never had to talk. These gunslingers were obviously bad men themselves, but they had been through a lot and often and were still alive. If you asked them why they still stuck together, each would have said the same thing.

If it ain't broke, don't fix it.

The shootists' rode side by side with the peasant across the dusty desert of Durango under the burning sun on the road to Santa Sangre.

The full moon hung faint as a ghost in the cloudless sky on the horizon, like a portent.

The trail curved higher around the upper ridge, and the riders slowed to a trot as the horses trod over the uneven ground. The peasant rode in the lead, followed by Tucker, then Bodie, then Fix in steady single-file formation.

They all heard the sudden shrill castanet.

The Mexican's horse violently reared, front legs bicycling, eyes wide in alarm, whinnying in terror. Its rider emitted a high-pitched scream of surprise, coming out of the stirrups as the mustang rose up on its hind legs in panic. A coiled rattlesnake tensed on the ground directly ahead, the rattler a twitchy blur as it shook its upraised tail, brown and copper head raised, jaw extended, fangs bared to strike. The startled peasant's horse pitched him from the saddle, arms and legs flailing, where he landed hard on the ground, inches in front of the rattler. The snake's narrow head was right by his contorted face, fangs curled and deadly sharp as it struck with vital speed.

The head of the reptile disappeared in a fine red mist, the headless red meat of its body dropping in a limp coil on the ground before the Mexican heard the gunshot explode across the desert.

The peasant screamed like a girl.

Fix had got his pistol out, fanned and fired so blindingly fast his gun was back in his holster before the dead and headless snake hit the ground.

The viper's rattle castaneted a final stubborn time, then fell silent and still in the settling dust.

The Mexican rose to his hands and knees, wiping splattered snake muck from his cheek with the back of his hand. His eyes raised to meet the cowboys in the saddles above him.

All three of the gunfighters gaped, looking down at the peasant.

The Mexican's shirt had come loose in the fall, and two ripe, nude brown breasts toppled out. With a gasp, she scooped her big naked bosom back into her baggy top, eyes wide in embarrassment and fear.

Now they all knew.

He was a she and a very beautiful she.

"Hello," Bodie said, with a slow dawning grin.

"Howdy, ma'am," Tucker said. He tipped his hat with a wink.

Fix grinned. "Lady, you'd a showed us them melons before, you could have kept the damn silver."

The hard men laughed coarsely, and the girl flinched in shame and dread. The gunfighters had ridden their horses to surround her on all sides, blocking her escape. Sitting high in their saddles, they were threateningly silhouetted against the mid-morning sun, the white orb blinding behind the sharp outlines of their Stetsons. Pilar crawled on her hands and knees, cringing with fear, expecting the worst.

In his saddle, Tucker saw what a pretty woman they had been with all morning and understood he'd known her gender all along. The glimpse of her breasts had gotten him aroused. Her round, high, big brown-nippled tits bounced real pretty when she loaded them back under her shirt. No question, on all fours there on the ground, surrounded by the three cowboys, she was theirs for the taking and maybe they'd get a little bonus with the silver. Tucker's eyes narrowed to circumspect slits as he glanced first across to Fix sitting on his horse staring with sardonic bemusement down at the cowering girl. Then his gaze slid over to Bodie in his saddle and that hungry look as the Swede's hand passed by his crotch giving it a tug. Tucker smelt the heat of rutting in the air like blood in the water and knew that all three of them could be down on the ground taking turns if he merely gave the word. They were miles from civilization in the middle of the desert and there was nowhere to run and nobody to come to her aid if they descended on the girl and had their way with her. But as the seconds passed, pragmatically, he thought better of it. They could ravish her now, but that would set them back a few hours and the girl might lose her mind and refuse to take them to the silver. Better to get to the silver first, then they could pound that brown body as much as they wanted. If she was that good looking, there might be a lot more fruit in her town ripe for picking.

In his mind, Tucker had the sudden image of a pack of coyotes, the hateful filthy mangy cowardly scavenger dogs circling their prey, closing in for the kill. At night, the shootists often heard the musical chorus of yipping in the distant hills, soon replaced by the inevitable horrible high-pitched cries of some terrified dying small dog or animal the miserable scavengers would lure out into the hills and then surround to ambush and slaughter, tearing it limb from limb. As the three dangerous men on their big horses circled the exposed, frightened, cringing girl crouching on the ground, Tucker saw the predatory glint in his friends' eyes as lust burned in their loins and the smell of sexual heat filled the dusty air. He knew they were the coyotes, nothing more than the lowest varmints.

It had come to this, then.

They had fallen that far, sunk to their lowest, become animals.

"No," Tucker mumbled first to himself, then repeated as an order he issued with quiet authority. "No, not like this, this ain't what we are, boys."

"Hey, honey, how 'bout you give my doorknob a little polish?" Bodie said, squeezing his crotch and making a move to unbutton his fly.

"Man has to relax." Fix grinned.

The girl shut her eyes and dropped her gaze, then opened them with flint in her bold stare as she grabbed a knife from her belt and held it protectively as she rose to her feet, ready to fight. She turned in a full circle, then back again, facing the gunfighters who loomed over her on their horses, ready to cut them if they made a move.

A twinge of conscience stirred in Tucker's heart. He felt sorry for the poor damn girl. This Mexican had pluck and smarts, and he understood the considerable tar it must have taken for a woman alone to have ridden out to save her village and stand toe to toe with hard-ass killers like the three of them were. He respected and liked her, right down to the ground.

"Shut up, boys, and step back," said Tucker. "Ain't no way to treat a lady. Let alone one who's payin' us."

Fix and Bodie exchanged reluctant glances and nodded, following orders.

"Do what the man says, Bodie. Get her horse," said Fix quietly.

The Swede nodded, trotting a few yards to where the riderless mustang stood casually grazing on a patch of mescal. He retrieved the dangling reins and led it right next to the girl.

Tucker kept his hands up, palms upraised to show he meant no harm, rode unthreateningly over with a clop of hooves, leaned down with a creak and clink of leather and stirrup and offered the girl a gloved hand to help her back into her saddle. The simple peasant considered him in surprise and confusion, naked fear and distrust in her gaze softening into raw relief as she slowly took his hand. Her knife remained in her other hand for a moment, then was returned to her belt as she let him grasp her small palm and tug her foot up into her stirrup and settle her back into the saddle of her horse. Now she was eye level with them, and Tucker held her gaze with gentlemanly grace. "We get it," he said. "You dressed yourself up as a man 'cause you didn't know the kind of men we were, and the kind of men you needed were the kind of men didn't need to know what y'had under them clothes. What's your name?"

"Pilar," she said, no longer trying to disguise her voice, her natural timbre pretty and chimelike.

"Pretty name."

Tucker grinned. She smiled, dropped her eyes, then raised them to meet his. "I am sorry. To deceive you. It is as you say."

"Hell, this day is getting more damn interestin' every minute. Never a dull moment, nossir," Fix said.

"And daylight's wasting if we're making this town by noon," said Bodie.

Tucker nodded. "Bodie's right. Let's ride."

As Pilar led the way, riding out of earshot on her shaken horse, Tucker shot a fierce glance to his fellow gunfighters. "Let's just get the silver, boys. Then we'll fuck her and her sisters."

"And her mother if'n she has a set of cans like that on her." Bodie winked.

They half meant it.

Spurring their horses, the four horses and riders surged across the plain.

Tucker knew they were being followed.

He could smell them.

It wasn't much to go on, just a wisp of dust behind them in the far distance, a faint metallic clink that could have been nothing at all somewhere way off. If they were riders, how many there were he couldn't tell. Durango was afflicted with sudden arid winds popping up and sweeping down the plains whipping up dust devils so he could not be sure. Except for the gnawing tension in his gut telling him someone was out there and closing in. They'd made no effort to conceal their horse tracks during the morning ride, so their sign was right out there for anybody to see.

Maybe they should have been more careful.

They better be mindful from now on.

The cowboy saw Fix catch him looking over his shoulder a few times, and they shared a glance that alerted the thin gunfighter in black there might be something on their ass and to be ready, but as usual they didn't need words. All the small, spare gunfighter did was slightly caress the pearl pistol handle in his holster with his worn black glove to protect his hand from the scrape of the hammer when he fanned and fired in the quick draw. The four riders continued into the sun-blasted oblivion.

The day was getting mean hot, and their destination lay hours ahead. Lizards scampered on rocks. Somewhere far off the razor *scree* of a hawk echoed into infinity. Then just the lulling clop of their hooves, and a waft of wind in his ears.

Bodie was in the rear, the giant Swede off in his own world, leaning back in his brown saddle, tree-stump legs relaxed, reins held loose in his cow-hoof hands, singing a loud song to himself in his gravelly, off-key voice. He grinned, bearing his cracked yellow teeth with sloppy affability, and laughed at some private joke in his granite boulder of a skull. He may be simple, Tucker felt, but he was so damn strong and there was an open-heartedness about him, so he didn't see the need to tell the big one about the riders who may or may not be shadowing the four. There was nothing to talk about yet, and Bodie would just forget the minute he was distracted by something shiny. Tucker was sometimes surprised the happy idiot remembered his name.

Ahead, the peasant girl led them along the barren trail, her black shiny close-cropped hair wafting in the wind, and her sweet floral scent drifted back to Tucker. For a few pleasant moments he just rode, closed his eyes, and breathed her in. This girl had sand. That she did. Again, he considered what it took for a young girl like her to recruit dangerous men like the three of them. She must have been very scared, but she'd done what she had to do. Where the hell were the men of her village? Goddamn Mexicans. Only one reason a simple girl like this would take the kind of risks she had. Whatever lay in wait for them at the town must be a hell of a lot scarier than they were. Tucker wanted to know the rest of the story and would ask her soon.

A huge cloud passed across the sun, creating a mile-long shadow that moved slowly across the desert like a scythe, the great darkness passing over them. It shadowed their faces beneath their hat brims in a black curtain against the bright daylight, making them squint. They all experienced a sudden chill, and then it was gone, replaced by the heat of the day as the overhead cloud passed the sun. The wall of shade continued on its relentless trek across the landscape like the shadow of the devil catching souls.

An antsy Tucker was getting tired of the ride. He just wanted to get there, to this town wherever it was, face up to whatever he was up against, do his killing and be done with it. The ride felt like an axe hanging over his head, the waiting worse than the battle. He knew he was a man of action because of this impatience and fierce nature. Waiting gave a man too much time to think and it wasn't good thinking too much.

"Hold up, boys."

For the third time on the last twenty miles Fix had found sign.

Tucker and Bodie pulled up their horses with Pilar, as the skeletal gunfighter in black bent from his saddle studying the ground. "I savvy fifteen sets of hoof prints," he said.

"What does this mean?" Pilar questioned, looking back and forth between her companions.

"Maybe somethin', maybe nothing," replied Fix. "They come in front from the north back at where we met up, then doubled back, crisscrossing their own tracks. Eight miles back, the tracks entered a shallow creek and didn't come out the other side, disappeared like, meaning them riders was heading in single-file formation through the water bed to disguise their movements, and when the creek turned into a river, too tough to negotiate with horses, the tracks finally came out."

"We ain't seen nobody." Bodie shrugged.

"Doesn't mean they ain't out there."

"Could be we're being followed," Tucker said.

"Let's keep our eyes peeled."

The peasant girl was worried. "Them, they are after you?"

The gunfighters looked at one another with a shared mutual understanding, but did not respond. It was an answer but no answer.

"Which them?" Bodie mumbled.

"Were you followed?" Tucker asked Pilar. "By whatever those varmints are holding your town?"

"I don't think so, Tuck," Bodie said. "We've been retracing her trail due south and Fix just said those tracks started from the north."

"We can sit around here scratching our balls talking about this all day. If we meet up with 'em we meet up with 'em. Let's get a move on," Tucker said.

His gang nodded. Pilar shrugged, and all four kept riding as the sun raised another few notches like the hand of a clock.

Fix, the signcutter of the bunch, noticed the stagecoach trail first.

It was two deep ruts in the ground heading east and west that he recognized as the Wells Fargo Durango route. They had happened onto it by accident. The cowboys briefly discussed following it, but Pilar insisted her village lay due south so off they set.

A mile away they came upon the stagecoach, or what was left of it.

The shattered wheel was the first thing they encountered, but the wreckage was not far off. The wagon had been completed destroyed. The carriage lay in an upside-down heaping pile of broken wooden boards and twisted metal chassis frame. The splintered doors, roof rack and spilled luggage were scattered debris all over the sunbaked rocks. The crushed skeletons of a team of dead horses were like one unrecognizable thing in a mountain of grinning skulls, spines, leg bones, hooves, horseshoes and caved-in rib cages jutting this way and that in a knotted confusion of harness and bridle, bleached clean in the merciless sun.

The horses they rode didn't like this, not one bit, and strained contrarily against their reins, protesting noisily and rearing so the men had to wrest them under control with a chorus of "woahs" and "easy." It was a bad place.

"Holy shit," muttered Bodie.

Tucker wondered what could have done this.

Pilar gazed on in knowing horror as the gunfighters took a few moments to ride around the wreckage, taking it all in.

"The stage must have been moving at a clip when it went off the road. What the hell was it doing driving this kind of terrain at that kind of speed? Must have been running from something." Tucker observed.

"It didn't just go off the road, boys. It got attacked," Fix added.

"The bandits around here don't mess around," Bodie said just to say something.

"If it was bandits, why didn't they rob it?" Fix nudged his jaw down at an open suitcase spilling clothes, a lady's purse and wad of cash on the ground. Sitting in his saddle, he drew out his carbine and held it by the stock, leaning down to pick up the valise using the long barrel. Confiscating the cash, he flung the empty purse and suitcase back into the dust. "Looks like this ride was already worth our time. We'll divvy this up later."

"How long you figure this wreck been here?"

"Judging by those bleached bones, a month, mebbe longer."

"You boys notice something strange?" Tucker mentioned, bothered, as he studied the rubble. "Where's the bodies?"

On the ground lay a shattered silver pocket watch on a broken length of small chain. Tucker picked it up and saw the words "John Whistler" engraved inside the bent lid. The name rang a bell and he remembered it belonged to a bounty hunter he had met up with years ago. For sure they would never meet again. The cracked glass cover of the time face showed the hour and minute hands frozen at 8:28, immortalizing the exact moment their owner departed the earth.

A ratty piece of paper fluttering in the dry arid wind caught his eye, and as it was picked up in the breeze he snatched it out of the air. The gunfighter perused it momentarily and squinted with agitation, and when he saw the others looking at him, he quietly passed the wanted poster with their faces on it around to the other two men to whom it pertained. When it got to Fix, the thin gunsel crumpled it in his fist and pocketed the wadded ball of paper before the girl got a look.

"Interestin'," he said.

"This watch belonged to John Whistler," Tucker observed. "That stage was heading in our direction and he was on it."

"Them wanted posters must've belonged to him," Bodie said, stating the obvious with a sense of discovery. "Two and two put together equals he was after the reward."

Tucker tossed away the broken pocket watch. It clattered on the rocks and lay still. "Reckon we should probably thank whoever took him out. Whistler was a real bad ass and could have given us big problems."

"I think we should say a few words over the dearly departed." Fix spat a blob of tobacco juice with precision accuracy, splattering the watch. "Fuck y'all. Amen."

"I know what did this," said Pilar. That was all she said.

"Let me guess," said Tucker. "Those we're goin' up against."

Her eyes told it all.

They rode on and left the decimated stagecoach in their dust.

67

Canyon cleaved up several hundred yards ahead, squeezing the trail into an ass crack of a ravine. The dull, tedious minutes passed as the three riders followed the horse of the determined peasant girl. One stallion exhaled with a wet *flubber*. The rattle of the packs on the saddles squeaked with leather over the clop of hooves as the men ascended the rise and came to a depression in the mesa baking like an oven under the nasty sun. The glare was so bright it hurt their eyes, and their vision swam as they squinted and visored their foreheads with their hands to shield their gaze from the sand that reflected like glass.

Ahead, a black smudge was in the watery waves of heat.

There were blurry dots in the sky in the molten, undulating thermals rising off the desert.

The closer they rode, they discerned those hovering spots were black birds. Vultures circling. Many.

Over the next hill, buzzards gathered.

An outpost.

The riders reined their horses.

Vultures continued their overhead circumference.

Over the ridge, the remains of a stagecoach station lay in smoldered ruins. The charred walls looked painted dull red, but on closer inspection the red was not paint.

"This is a bad place," whispered the girl. "*Muy mal.*"

The gunfighters dismounted their horses and drew their irons.

"Easy, boys. This place ain't right," Tucker said.

Fix sniffed. "You boys smell that?"

"Like an open grave." Bodie winced.

The three cowboys carefully approached the gutted ruins of the stage junction a hundred yards before them. The lonely building sat quietly in an open clearing with nothing for miles but a few yucca plants and the worn rutted trail running past it. Tucker led, eyes glued to the area, gesturing with his fingers for the others to come forward when he saw the coast was clear. The building was a one-story brick construction with a wooden porch and a paddock.

There had been a great disturbance. Saddles and tack lay scattered on the ground, thrown to and fro as if in a savage rage. One of the saddles was raked with four ragged claw marks that had cut deep into the leather, shredding and nearly shearing it in half. The outpost had clearly been torched from the inside, and Bodie kicked away a broken melted kerosene lamp that may have been the cause. There was no sign of life, no movement at all. Just the three figures of the heavily armed gunfighters coming at it on three sides, pistols at the ready, their gun barrels following their noses. The silence was oppressive, the opposite of sound, a vacuum that felt like it sucked them all in. The men moved steadily forward in a low crouch and passed the corral when they were assailed by a sudden overpowering stench.

Behind the fence, the bleached white skeletons of six dead horses lay in a heaping pile on the ground, their skulls and leg bones torn completely off their bodies, and rib cages broken open to reveal open black holes of their gut cavities. Long, dragging tears of teeth and claw marks marred their skeletal remains. Clouds of flies swarmed in the eyes and mouths of the dead horses' craniums. Globular eye sockets gaped as if from the unimaginable agony of the horrific way they died.

"They didn't have to kill them horses," growled Fix, who hated cruelty to animals though he didn't admit it.

"They didn't just kill them. They scourged them," observed Tucker. "You boys know any Injun tribes this area do that, a warning mebbe?"

The stretched equine jawbones and jutting teeth were contorted in death's head grimaces. Some of their dried guts hung draped from the rails of the paddock. The stench of old rot and bile was overpowering.

"None I ever heard of. And this ain't Injun land."

"Could be a war party," added Bodie.

"I don't know what the hell this is. Exceptin' that this is Mexico."

69

They hunkered by the edge of the corral abattoir and considered the porch to the outpost a few paces ahead. Huge streaks of black char rose up the adobe walls by the splashes of clotted blood as if buckets of gore had been tossed against the structure. The roof beams were incinerated.

Tucker looked back and saw the peasant girl riding closer after her initial trepidation. The look on her face was not as frightened as he would have expected from a plain and simple girl, it was like she had seen this all before.

"Stay back," he called to her.

Shaking her head, the peasant warily climbed off her horse and followed the men as they approached the ominous stagecoach junction. The doors and windows were black and foreboding like the sockets of a skull.

Death was here.

Movement in the doorway darkness caused the three gunfighters to raise their weapons, ready to fire.

With a bitter caw, five filthy buzzards exploded out the open door and beat a sickening ascent into the searing bleached sky.

The gunslingers entered the outpost, guns leveled.

Inside the structure, Tucker and Bodie stared at what lay before them in raw horror and these men had seen it all. Even Fix's eyes bugged out of his head, finger sweaty on his trigger. The large room was dark and gloomy, bright sunlight cutting through the musty air in big shafts that revealed the inside of the building was washed floor to roof with clotted blood. Countless flies were stuck to the dried gore, wings twitching. The decayed skeletons of several people dangled from ropes on the ceiling, hung from their feet, bones rattling in the dry breeze. Swarming flies buzzed.

"Hellfire," Fix whispered.

The cowboys covered their noses with their kerchiefs, wincing at the horrible stench, their squinty eyes regarding the ghastly scene, then each other.

Several piles of bones were assembled around the dirt floor. These people had been passengers, waiting for the stage but meeting up with something else instead. The skulls and femurs were immediately recognizable as human. The skeletons had been gnawed clean, and those tidy piles were neat, deliberate. Clothes were heaped in another pile, black with dried blood, so the victims had been stripped after they were killed. Tucker gauged there were maybe eight to ten sets of human remains. Two of the skulls were very small and delicate, a child and an infant, both crushed in like porcelain dolls. A stuffed teddy bear Tucker guessed belonged to one of the children sat slumped over on a wooden table, its black button eyes blank as if erased by what it had witnessed. He saw a heap of emptied suitcases and carpetbags piled in the corner by the small stove. The luggage had been rifled through, valuables filched, robbed. The work of bandits, likely, from the looks of things, but what kind of bandits would do this to people defied comprehension. Then again, Tucker didn't know these parts, and maybe these looters had showed up after whomever had done the killing. A dead, half-smoked cigar sat on a rusted metal horseshoe ashtray, probably still burning when the killers came. Tucker picked up the stogie, put it in his mouth, and lit it. The smoke drifted out of his lips, and helped wash away the carrion stink of the place as he looked around.

Fix kicked at a buzzard waddling in.

"Awww God, they killed kids, poor little kids didn't do nothin'."

Alerted by the distress in Bodie's voice, Tucker slid his eyes over to see the towering Swede crouching under the low roof, his cement-block face crumpled in a distraught expression, huge hands holding the tattered, blood-drenched lace and frill homemade dress of a little girl now just gruesome rags in his thick fingers. The cloth slipped through his hands, dropping with an empty sound on the sodden dirt. Tucker watched the despondent Bodie run his hand in dismay through his hair, clenching and unclenching his repeater rifle in the other until his knuckles grew big and white as pebbles. This was the worst thing any of them had ever seen. The leader felt it too, the same rage they all did, and knew as his friends did that if they came face to face with those responsible, the gunfighters would kill them real slow, shoot them apart piece by piece and watch them die screaming in their own blood and shit all day long. Then they'd cut their heads off and put them on sticks. They'd done it before.

"Those was bad kills," Fix said.

"Them people was skinned alive," muttered Tucker.

Bodie shook his head. "Goddamn massacre. Never seen nothing like it. Ever."

"You figure it was the same sumbitches in this town we're going up against?" Fix worked his jaw.

Tucker nodded. "Reckon."

"Scalphunters?" Fix spat.

"Nope." Tucker shook his head, fingering his beard. He indicated the messy mops of grisly matted pelt on some of the faceless skulls. "They'd have took the hair."

"Right."

Bodie shrugged. "Coyotes, then? Rabid mebbe?"

"Open your eyes, Bodie. Look." Fix bristled at the other gunfighter's stupidity. "They's hung from the rafters."

Tucker glowered. "Pulled apart limb from limb while they were alive, too, from the looks of things." He hunkered down by the piles of arm bones pulled off the dangling skeletons and grimaced at the teeth marks gnawed to the marrow. "And eaten."

"Eaten?" Bodie squirmed squeamishly.

Fix stared impassively. "Nobody should die like that."

Taking off his hat, shaken to the core, the wiry little gunfighter went outside for air. The other two gunslingers remained, legs weak, as if the empty eye sockets and grinning teeth of *los deparacedos*, the disappeared ones, wished them to bear witness a few moments longer.

"Who would do something like this?" Tucker whispered mostly to himself.

"It was them, *señors.*" The girl stood in the doorway, her arms crossed, her honest gaze grim.

"This was what come to your town?" Fix asked from outside.

"*Si.*"

Bodie whistled.

"Then lady, you got some big problems," Tucker grunted.

"That's why I have you," the peasant answered, a fact simply stated. And he thought he might have seen her smile, just a little.

"What the hell have we gotten ourselves into?"

"Boys," muttered Fix. "I found sign."

The cowboys went outside, glad to get out of the slaughterhouse. The abattoir of an outpost sat festering in the light of day. The vultures, afraid of the armed men, hung back, impatient for them to depart so they could resume their feast.

Tucker and Bodie walked up to Fix, who had squatted down on one knee a dozen yards away by a huge amount of horse tracks heading away from the outpost due south.

"Must be them." Fix looked up. "Heading away from us."

"They came here before our town. The first night we heard them it was from the north." Pilar fought tears. "You see? You see what will happen to my people if you don't help us? Please help us, *señors*. Please."

Tucker nodded. "That's what you hired us for, ma'am. But we better get a move on."

They saddled up. All four spurred their horses hard, getting the hell out of there and urging the animals full gallop until they were long gone over the next ridge. The ghastly outpost and its congregation of buzzards fell out of sight, if not out of mind, to their rear. The dry, raw wind of the open desert in their faces washed the stench of death from their noses and mouths, but the taste lingered, until at last they let up on their horses and slowed to a canter on the dusty trail.

CHAPTER FIVE

AS THEY RODE ON, TUCKER LOOKED OVER HIS SHOUL-
der and saw the distant dust trail of a group of horses and riders
on their tail.

Fix looked back too with a furrowed brow. "What is it?"

Tucker squinted. "Mebbe something. Mebbe nothing."

When they looked again, there was no sign of anything behind.
Bodie's hand went to his pistol in his holster. "We got trouble?"

Tucker shook his head. "Nah. Outpost back there rattled me some
is all."

They didn't ride far when Bodie whistled. "Boys, we got company."

The two other gunfighters looked up to see what their fellow
shootist was eyeballing.

Back about a mile off, through the melting waves of rising heat, a
wall of riders was coming in their direction, kicking up dust.

"That who I think it is?"

Tucker nodded. "I'd bet money. Let's get out of here." The men
spurred their horses and took off.

The girl started her horse to gallop in order to keep up. "Why are
we riding so fast?" she hollered.

Tucker yelled to her over the pounding hooves. "We need to make time to get to your town!"

A maze of granite canyon breaks lay directly ahead. A piece of luck. The cowboys and the girl made for them. A labyrinth of gray mud arroyos and gulleys networked the valley for the next few miles, big enough to ride horses through. They might lose their pursuers in there. The cowboys and the peasant trotted down a steep narrow draw until it spilled out in a wending ravine that tooled through the cool high rock walls thirty feet above them. Their hooves splashed through a thin stream of water flowing by. They didn't look back, just forged ahead, as the bend went right, then left, then right again. There was no sign of it spilling out, or even an indication of where it led. Tucker understood while the canyon breaks offered an escape route in which they could lose those after them, the gunfighters were also trapped, boxed in. If they got cornered their backs were to the wall. Worse, if their adversaries were up above on the top of the ridge and spotted them riding down in the ravine, they would have the high ground and pick them off easily. A quick glance at the worried looks on his fellow gunfighters' faces and Tucker saw they were thinking the same thing. Fix certainly was. That damn Bodie was probably thinking about grub. It was a double-edged sword being down here, and Tucker wondered whether it had been a mistake. That was when he heard the sound of hoof beats, a great many, echoing down in the latticework of ravines with them. He knew then that he didn't have to worry about these pursuers being up on the ridge, because they were right down there with them and would catch up directly.

"Lock and load," he snarled.

"Good. I'm getting sick of this running crap," said Fix.

"We don't know how many they are," shot back Tucker. "There's no money in mixin' it up with these whoever-they-ares, plus we got silver to get to and best save our bullets for that. I say we lose 'em."

"I'm with Tucker." Bodie nodded.

They pulled up their horses and stopped at a fork in the canyon. Dark, craggy, twisting ravines broke off in three directions. The muffled echo of the hooves of many riders loudly reverberated seemingly from all directions, a sound like a rushing river, rebounding off the walls of chipped rock rising thirty feet above them.

"There's a lot of 'em. But I'm ready," panted Bodie.

"Which way?" snarled Fix, pulling up his reins and urgently looking left and right down the empty ravines leading off in opposite directions into the canyons. The sound of horses was growing in volume, more distinct, but it was impossible to tell which way they were coming at them from. Pilar tossed her head as she gazed around her, face sweating and beautiful with alarm.

"I don't know," Tucker growled through gritted teeth, pump shotgun in one hand and reins in the other as he turned his horse in a circle, listening. He shot a desperate glance upward at the notch of the top of the pass. "Find a trail leading up to the top of the canyon, then we get the high ground and shoot down at 'em."

"Where?" shouted Fix.

"This way."

Pilar was wild with fear, hunched in her saddle. "It is *them, señors!*"

"No, not them." Tucker dug his spurs into his stallion's flanks. "Let's go!"

The ridge lay ahead in the daylight. The men charged for the hill. They almost made it when six Federales galloped their horses around the edge of the canyon to suddenly surround them on all sides, hooves sending up clouds of flying dirt and pebbles. The grizzled, tough men wore dusty tan uniforms and were armed to the teeth. Their button coats were crisscrossed with rifle straps. Each had a tan cap on their heads. The knee-high black boots, brass buckles and spurs glinted in the sun. The soldiers already had pistols drawn, and a few had rifles to their shoulders.

"*Halto!*" their Captain yelled. He was a swarthy, gaunt man with military bearing and a sunken, oily aspect to his countenance.

The gunfighters quickly circled their horses, hands by their guns, braced for action.

Tucker looked up and nudged his chin at his friends and they followed his gaze. Thirty feet above them, on the cliff of the ravine, more Federales rose into position, rifles aimed down their noses at the gunfighters' heads.

"Easy," he said to Fix and Bodie. They were way outnumbered and outgunned.

"Mornin." Tucker clenched his jaw and regarded the beady-eyed comandante.

Pilar spoke up first, words in Spanish tumbling out of her pretty mouth as she plaintively implored the impassive Federales, gesturing her hands emotively. Tucker only knew a little of the local language, but thought he caught something about bandits and a town and protection, and he figured she was explaining they were with her to help save her people. But then she rode up too close to the Captain and he struck her silent with a brutal swipe of the back of his gloved hand. She just cringed in her saddle, watching him and the other soldiers with fear and despair.

The three gunslingers reacted in a rage that surprised them, a bond already formed with the girl they had just met that morning, and in unison their hands moved an inch dangerously closer to their holstered weapons.

There was a resounding chorus of ratcheting *clicks* of hammers being drawn back on the guns of the soldiers surrounding them, and the cowboys thought better of reckless action.

Tucker clenched his jaw. "You didn't have to do that, asshole."

"*Que?*" the martinet replied.

Fix squinted. "Something we can help you boys with?"

The Federale Captain barked, "What are your names?"

"Smith," said Bodie.

"Jones," said Fix.

"Abraham Lincoln," replied Tucker.

The comandante squinted and pulled a folded wanted poster out of his jacket, looking it over. Pilar watched the soldiers and the gunslingers in alarm, her eyes tensely dodging back and forth. The cowboys exchanged slow, laconic, loaded glances. Fix's jaw slowly worked his chewing tobacco. The Federale officer passed the wanted poster to his Sergeant, who displayed it.

Recognizable likenesses of Tucker, Bodie and Fix's faces were on the paper.

Pilar glanced back at her fierce hirelings to see what they were going to do and what they did visibly surprised her. Tucker started to chuckle, and he was joined by Fix and then Bodie, and now they were all three laughing and then the Captain's fat lips split and he was laughing too, until his medals-laden chest shook, and now all the soldiers in the canyon were laughing like it was one big joke. But Pilar knew it was not funny and people were about to die very badly.

Fix spat a glob of tobacco juice on the poster.

The Federale Captain went for his gun.

Like one deadly killing machine, the gunfighters quickdrew their pistols from their side holsters, amazingly fast, blowing the Captain clean out of his saddle. Dismounted, the Federale seemed to Pilar to float in the air forever, arms and legs twirling, big flowers of blood and jetting gore erupting from the holes in his chest. Even bigger discharges of red meat out his back splattered the faces of the soldiers behind him, even as their heads disappeared in a disintegration of hair and skull. The ventilated comandante finally hit the ground and lay still in a great cloud of settling dust.

By then the air was alive with flying bullets that boomed and buzzed and whined around the canyon like furious bees. Lightning and thunder burst from the muzzles of the gunfighters' irons as they fanned and fired, again and again, in every direction.

Pilar cowered in abject terror as her horse reared and pawed the air, turning on its hind legs as she grabbed onto the saddle for dear life to stop from sliding off, but the girl toppled from the panic-stricken animal's rump onto the hard ground and smashed her shoulder. When she looked up, framed against the sun she saw the titanic behemoth of her horse on its back legs over her. Its powerful shod hooves came down on the ground directly at her head. Pilar rolled away as two slugs ricocheted off the ground in an ear-shattering din that cut her scalp with chips of rock. The horse's hooves crashed down by her head, and she lay flattened on the earth seeing only the exploding bullets and the rampaging legs of many horses. She saw a set of familiar hooves charging straight for her and curled in a ball covering her head, cursing herself for her weakness, knowing she was about to be trampled to death, failing her people.

It was going to hurt to die.

But that didn't happen.

The horse thundered past her as a hand grabbed her arm and pulled with amazing strength. It heaved her like a feather up off the ground and over her rescuer's saddle, shielding her head with his shoulders and chest. Pilar knew his scent, the good smell of the one called Tucker.

The horse steered around, and the cowboy carefully placed her on the ground behind a large boulder at the edge of the raging gunfight. As her feet touched solid earth, she looked up at the gunfighter in his saddle and saw the flash of kindness in his wild, concerned eyes.

"Stay down!" he roared.

The girl nodded, breathless.

With that, his spurred horse charged around the boulder back into the fray, him holding onto the saddle with his knees as both hands held pistols and the guns belched fire, over and over.

Pilar covered her ears and peered around the edge of the rock, watching it all go down. A thrill of excitement such as she had never experienced filled her while she gazed on, transfixed. The shooting raged in a frenetic chaos of horses and men and flying slugs that she saw unfold with intense detail.

The jaw of one of the soldiers was shot off.

Another took a bullet in the eye.

Now some had abandoned their horses to seek cover behind the rocks. Up on the ridge, two soldiers leaped up from cover, silhouetted against the sun. They traded fire with Fix, then Tucker.

Tucker quickly crisscrossed his arms, aiming his left-handed gun over his right shoulder and his right-handed pistol over the left, firing upward twice, toppling two of the Federales off the cliffs above them. The men fell screaming, trailing ropes of blood until they hit the rocks with a wet *splat*. Tucker had whirled his horse around and was firing two-fisted and straight-armed at three other soldiers who blasted back with their rifles. His pistols empty, Tucker holstered them and in one smooth move withdrew a pump shotgun from his saddlebag. He raised it to his shoulder, one hand holding down the trigger while the hand on the pump jerked back and forth in a blasting motion that never ceased. Sparks and flashes ricocheted everywhere on the canyon walls. The Federales fell.

Pilar watched enthralled from the ground behind the boulder. She had not seen these gunslingers fight until now, and had never seen men such as these in action. They moved like one weapon, and it was a dance of lethal beauty. Now she knew what they could do.

In the midst of the battle, Fix got off his horse, gave the skittish animal a smack on its rump sending it on its way bolting out of the melee, and stood on his own two feet. He seemed more comfortable that way. The little gunfighter just held his ground, terrifyingly still, as bullets flew around him, calmly placing his aim and surgically picking off soldiers. Pilar observed that Fix made few moves, measuring every gesture, and that his very stillness and implacability under fire rattled his enemies. They hesitated a second too long to take proper aim, and by then the unblinking little man had them targeted and his slug was in flight. Bullets whined past him, but he didn't flinch. He was scary, dressed incongruously in the soiled black gentlemen's vest, suit and bowler hat.

Bodie's horse was hit in the head by a stray round and went down, spilling the giant Swede out of his saddle. Both came to earth with a great crash. He pushed the heavy, dead stallion off him with one hand. Grabbing up his Winchester, he waded into the skirmish on foot with a great roar of fury and a very big grin.

Tucker had been hit.

She didn't see when it had happened but now his face was screwed up in pain as he held a bleeding puddle of red on his arm, though it didn't seem to stop him as he yanked off his handkerchief and with a quick tugging motion tourniqueted his arm tightly. The soldier who had shot him needed to reload and was bathed in desperate sweat fumbling fresh rounds into his pistol. Without missing a beat, the bearded gunslinger one-handed his pump shotgun with his unimpaired hand and blew the soldier clean away. Catapulted back a good twenty feet through the air against the side of a cliff, the Federale slid down the wall, sliming a snail trail of blood, already a corpse.

Whirling her head, Pilar saw Bodie swinging his rifle by the barrel like he was swatting at flies, clubbing the soldiers in the heads, emptying their skulls as they dropped like sacks.

Then suddenly, they were the last men standing. Half-visible in an eldritch ether of gunsmoke and dust, Tucker, Fix and Bodie stood tall and still on the body-strewn ground, the three men fearsomely silhouetted in the haze that hung in the air. Pilar watched them from behind the boulder, her heart pounding in her bosom. It was over.

These were terrifying men.

Who was it she had hired?

What had she unleashed?

True, the blue-eyed one had risked his life to shield her body with his own when the shooting had begun, had gotten her to safety and had not thought twice. Yet what of the others, she worried, maybe they were worse. Then she remembered what her father always said.

You can tell a man by the company he keeps.

She didn't know here if that was a good thing or a bad thing.

One thing Pilar was sure of.

She had chosen well.

The gunslingers holstered their pistols and looked around. The ground was littered with uniformed corpses. They'd gotten them all, of that Tucker was certain. The wanted poster wafted in the wind, riddled with holes. His arm smarted, but a quick once over showed the bullet had gone clean through, so he tightened the scarf tourniquet and figured he'd tend to the wound when they got to the town in a few hours. They must be close now. Looking at Fix and Bodie he saw they were all right.

The taut little mustached gunfighter was wandering among the corpses, giving them the long eyeball. He stopped by one, fingered his lip hair, and then patted the dead body down for valuables, feeling around the pockets.

Bodie had already gotten busy gathering their horses from across the ravine where they had bolted. The giant was selecting a fresh bay from one of the dead Federale's mounts since his own horse had been felled. He led the animals across the gully, soothingly patting their flanks with his great hands and making comforting sounds, and there he tied them off. Then Bodie walked to where his horse lay dead, bleeding from the head. Getting down on one knee, crestfallen, he untied the belts of his saddle with his sausage fingers and removed it. Shoulders slumped, he carried his saddle back toward their tethered horses and began to tack his new horse.

Looking the other way, Tucker saw Pilar rising from behind the rock, shaken but with a look of great relief on her face. He gestured to her it was safe to come out and she approached, looking down at all the dead men and crossing herself again and again. That was the first time he noticed the small silver crucifix on the delicate chain around her neck. The peasant eyed the hard gunmen with naked awe, respect and horror. She was probably wondering who the hell she got in bed with, he figured.

"Daylight's wasting. Let's ride," grunted Tucker.

"Not yet," Fix said.

The small, wiry, flinty-eyed cowboy hunkered in a crouch, rummaging efficiently through the cadavers' clothes, stealing money off the dead Federales. He used his gunstock to knock out the gold teeth of one carcass and pocketed his grisly bounty. "They won't be needin' none of that *dinero*." Fix made a brisk, tidy search of the other corpses' clothes in a matter of minutes. The peasant was mortified. When the little man had stuffed his pockets full of coins, wallets, loose bills and bloody, glinting metal teeth, he wandered over to his horse and dumped the spoils of the kill into one of his saddlebags. "We'll divvy up at the town."

"Least you left the hair," Tucker snorted.

"This time." Fix grinned.

"Let's go," grunted the leader.

They moved to their horses.

The Mexican knelt by the bodies, waving her arms. "No, *señors*. We must bury them."

"What?" said Fix.

"It is only right," Pilar said, as if it was plain common sense. She got up and brushed off her knees. "They must have words spoken over them."

Bodie laughed and spat. "Here's some words for 'em . . . See ya, wouldn't wanna be ya." The cowboys all had a good laugh at that.

"Thought you said we need to get to your town by noon," said Tucker softly.

Pilar shook her head devoutly, and he knew they had a situation. "Those who fell must be buried or it is a mortal sin. We need God on our side in the hours ahead and this is a test of our faith." The girl stood with her hands clasped by her stomach facing them patiently as she stood among the bodies, and the three cowboys watched her as they stood with their hands on the saddles of their horses.

"You're shittin' me." Fix's eyes widened in incredulity.

"I don't think she is." Tucker chuckled, shaking his head to himself as he looked down his rangy frame at his boots.

The peasant gestured to battlefield. "It will not take much time, if we all dig."

Bodie laughed. "Us? Dig?"

The peasant girl nodded with a sweet, hopeful smile.

"I ain't lifting a finger," Fix snorted.

"Leave 'em to the buzzards," agreed Bodie.

"No, no, no. . .!" Pilar shook with distress.

Tucker lowered his voice to a reasonable tone. "Sister, these bastards tried to kill us. They were bad men. They'd have left us for dead. They can rot."

"Señors, they were Federales."

"Trust us, those swine wasn't no kind of law," Tucker sighed.

Fix bristled with anger and impatience. "Woman, you are getting on the worse side of our better nature."

Bodie growled restlessly. "We're riding out of here now, says us."

The small, pretty girl sighed and stubbornly grabbed a small hand shovel from her saddle with soft resolve. Her shoulders slumped, she walked to the ground near the dead bodies and started to dig. "I understand, *señors*. I will do it. It will not take too long." Then she began shoveling dirt.

Tucker tipped his hat. "Knock yourself out."

As the peasant dug away, the cowboys loitered fifty yards away and passed the time watching the girl toil diligently without complaint. It took her about ten minutes to unearth the first shallow grave about three feet deep out of the mud which was soft and damp from the creek running through the canyons. Already she sweated from the heat and the effort. The three gunfighters watched her with bored and casual disinterest from the shade of a nook in the granite wall where they had tethered the horses. Tucker had a smoke, then rolled another. Pilar grabbed the dead Federale Captain by the feet, the only way she could move his weight, and tugged the body toward the open grave. His uniform was red with blood, ragged holes of cloth and flesh in the torso by the medals. With a grunt of exertion, she kneeled down and rolled his body over into the ditch with a dull wet *thud* of flopping limbs. She said a few hushed words over the deceased and kissed her crucifix. Then Pilar rose, grabbed the shovel and scooped the pile of dirt back in the hole onto his body with a steady *thump* of impact. When she was done five minutes later, she tamped the dirt on the mound of the shallow grave and set directly to work digging the next.

Eight more bodies lay sprawled.

The day moved on atop the ridge.

The sun was higher in the sky.

The peasant had two graves dug. Working on the third, she was lathered in sweat. But tired as she was, she did not fail to clasp her crucifix over each buried soldier and quietly whisper a few words. The nearby cowboys saw her lips enunciate but they couldn't hear her. The three gunfighters lounged impatiently by their horses, cleaning their guns. All of them were antsy. "How many those Federales you boys figure that *señorita* is gonna plant before she tires out?" Fix asked, jaw working a plug of tobacco in annoyance.

"Wench is plumb set to keel over right now." Bodie waved a big paw dismissively.

"So how many more bodies you figure, Tuck?"

"All of 'em." Tucker smiled, fondly watching the distant shapely figure forging on. The woman had brass, that she did. "All of 'em."

Big mile-long cloud shadows moved across the ridge, shadowing the cowboys' faces under the shaded brims of their hats. In the passing darkness, it became cool as the temperature dropped by degrees. When the clouds passed, the sun was higher yet, hotter and burning down.

Four graves. One tired Mexican. Still shoveling.

The cowboys lay on the ground with their hats over their eyes. They exchanged glances, feeling like swine. They regarded the peasant girl. Fix yelled, "Hurry it up there, missy!"

They looked at one another.

Tucker nudged his jaw to the other gunfighters. "Give her some water, boys."

Bodie grabbed a canteen. "Little lady, drink this so you don't die on us, 'fore we get that silver." Pilar gratefully caught the canteen, took a thirsty swig, tossed it back and returned to work on the fourth grave.

Tucker regarded the others evenly. He felt like a no account letting the girl do all that work, not lifting a hand to help her. While he didn't care about the corpses, she did and that's what mattered. At least he could show some manners and get off his ass. "Savvy mebbe we should help her," he muttered.

Fix bunched his shoulders, lowering his head under his bowler hat stubbornly. "Hell, it's her thing, let her do it."

Tucker looked to the sky. "We're burnin' daylight. Sooner them graves get dug the sooner we get to that silver."

Bodie scoffed. "Daylight, hell. You're just feeling sorry for the damn little twist." The gunfighters watched the exhausted peasant struggling under her labors.

"So shoot me." The leader got up and grabbed a hand shovel from his saddle, resigned. He joined Pilar digging the grave, using one arm mostly, and the appreciative girl grinned prettily as a desert flower.

It went quicker.

The other two cowboys watched from across the gulley. Fix gave in to peer pressure first. "I don't want to hear it, Bodie." With a resentful grunt, the small shootist clambered to his dusty boots, got his shovel and joined the impromptu gravediggers.

Bodie yelled across the area at them. "You're dumb shits, both of you, hear me! I ain't digging. Nossir, not me! Bury them heathen sumbitches tried to kill us? Screw that! They wouldn't have done for us, that's for damn sure. You boys listenin' to me?" His pals ignored him, putting their backs into shoveling. Bodie turned beet red, embarrassed. "You go right on digging. See if I care! You boys are goin' soft! Soft. You hear me? I am just going to sit back here on this hot ground and drink whisky and get drunk and laugh at you fools! That's what I'm gonna do. Ha ha! That's me laughin'. Want to hear more? Ha ha! I ain't diggin' no graves for no sumbitches! I am just gonna sit right here on my ass." He took a slug of hootch. "Damn your eyes."

Grumbling, Bodie got up, grabbed his shovel and joined his fellow gunslingers digging the graves.

The lovely peasant girl was happy and flashed them her beautiful white teeth. "You are good men, *señors*."

"Shut up!" The three cowboys shouted at her in unison.

The Mexican was smiling anyway.

The desert was bright under the light of midday and the clouds had moved off, leaving the sky white as bleached bone by the time the four horses disappeared in the distance.

Nine shallow mounds behind them in the dirt.

CHAPTER SIX

THE *BORRACHO'S* NAME IS HECTOR VARGAS BUT FAR back as he can remember people called him The Drunk.

So be it.

Thinking he never liked his name anyway, he sits in the saddle and rides into town on his horse for a place he seeks. The harsh sun is raw and hot overhead, burning down on his face under his sombrero. The old man is armed to the teeth with the guns and ammo stolen from the dead Federales back at the jail, but doesn't expect trouble. The place looks quiet and is not much of a town to begin with.

He trots past the cantina where the gunfighters met up with the peasant girl that very morning, but that means nothing to him for he does not know them.

It has been a month since the werewolf broke him out of his cell and he'd hit the trail with the arms, silver and horse stolen from the police station. The *borracho* still wears the same shabby raggedy man clothes that are much dustier now, the blood on them from that fateful night long since dried. For weeks he has drifted around Durango, drinking up much of the silver, but he still has plenty left and will need it. A disturbing dream the old man has been having since his escape tells him what he must do and this is why he is here. A full cycle of the moon has passed since he shot the werewolf and tonight the moon will be full again, so he does not have time to waste. The lives of many depend on him.

His horse passes the run-down structures of the tiny town one by one, silent and still in the hazy dust. The quiet *clop* of his *caballo's* hooves in the dirt are all he hears. The old man's leathery sunburned face turns side to side as he rides, his squinting eyes searching for the establishment he knows must be here, for every town has one.

At last he finds it. The gunsmith works out of a small barn in back of the stables. The *borracho* tethers his horse in the paddock, takes his confiscated rifles, pistols and bag of silver and enters. It is cooler inside the store, but not by much, and the old man wipes sweat with his handkerchief. Guns, feed and horse oats stack the racks. The emaciated Mexican proprietor looks up at him with suspicion, giving the stink eye to his derelict appearance and the weapons he carries. The drunk sees the owner reach defensively for an unseen gun under the counter and quickly puts the bag of silver in front of him so the man knows he means business, not robbery.

The proprietor eyes the silver in the pouch, then its grizzled owner. "How can I help you?"

"I need you to make me bullets."

"We sell ammo. Every caliber."

"I need you to make me bullets of silver."

Crazy old man, say the storekeeper's eyes.

"For these weapons," the *borracho* adds, placing the bolt-action rifle, repeater rifle and two revolvers on the counter.

"You want me to make silver bullets?"

"As many as this amount of silver will produce. Minus your payment, of course." His crusty, gnarled fingers pour the silver coins out of the pouch and push aside a small fortune, sliding it over. That still leaves many, many coins for the job. For the first time, the proprietor smiles. Shiny metal glints in his eyes in the dusty sunlight drifting through the windows.

"I can do that," the gunsmith says. Picking up the four weapons the *borracho* provides, he dutifully checks out their calibers one after the other. ".22. .45. .476. Do you have a preference?"

"Make as many bullets as you can manufacture for all of them."

It will take him an hour. Make yourself comfortable, the owner tells his unusual customer. Have a drink, in fact take the bottle, you are paying me enough, he says. So the old man takes a seat on a barrel keg and rests his tired bones for what he knows will be a long hard ride ahead if he is to make his destination by sundown. The bottle is gladly accepted, its contents drained for fortitude.

He will need all the liquid courage he can muster.

The proprietor melts down the silver on a pan over a pot-bellied stove in back of the store. He is friendly now and curious, and asks questions the old man softly answers.

"You are going to sell these bullets?"

"No, I am going to use them."

"Pardon me, *señor*, but you don't look like a *pistolero*."

"I am a drunk. A *borracho*."

"Why the silver bullets?"

"You would not believe me."

"It's your money."

"I have something I must make right."

While the gunsmith makes the bullets the old man goes outside and waters his horse for the journey.

And an hour later it is done.

The silver is melted down then poured into bullet-head molds, which are hardened in ice water to be inserted into cartridge casings of the required caliber after the gunpowder. One hundred eighty-nine bullets in all.

"What is your name, stranger?"

"I am Hector Vargas."

And today I will do what must be done.

"Good luck to you, Señor *Hector*. When I hear of silver bullets, I will know of your deeds." The drunk takes the shiny ammo and nods thanks.

The gunsmith has come to like the sad, strange old man and helps him load his weapons, for the drunkard's hands shake. The shop owner feels a twinge of remorse watching through the window as the *borracho* struggles into the stirrups of his horse and rides off. He reckons the man that bought the silver rounds will surely be shot dead by a regular lead bullet before he ever gets a chance to pull his own trigger.

The *borracho* learned the purpose of silver bullets from his grandfather when he was just a boy. None of the people in the town believed The Men Who Walked Like Wolves existed. They thought his grandfather a drunken fool, but the aged farmer swore it had been written by the Old Ones that silver was the only way to kill them.

His grandfather had also taught Hector how to drink, letting the lazy boy take his first sips of whisky from his bottle when he was ten. One day, the young *borracho* had accompanied his father's father on a ride in their cart from their village to a nearby town to fetch supplies. "Take this useless *nino*," his father had said. "Hector is no good for work here." That suited the boy fine because he hated hard labor and loved his crazy *abuelo*. Off they rode, leaving the village far behind. Passing the bottle back and forth in the shaky wagon, they rode through the desert in the hot sun and it was a good day. The trek should have taken just hours, but their horse broke a leg in a rut by late afternoon. The boy cried as his grandfather told him not to look and there was a single gunshot and the lamed *caballo* lay dead in the sand.

It was many miles to town and almost as far back to the village, so his grandfather said they would spend the night under the stars and start on foot in the morning.

It was a bad decision.

There was a full moon that night.

The dark desert was cold and they shared the blanket and the bottle that was running low. *Abuelo*, the boy had asked, are not werewolves about? His grandfather had smiled, told him not to worry for they were protected, and this was when he displayed the fistful of silver-headed cartridges he took from his pocket. Dumping the regular bullets from the cylinder of his *pistola*, he loaded the SAA revolver with the shiny ones that glinted bright in the moonlight. The young *borracho* saw his grandfather cock the pistol and set it by his side as he lay in the back of the cart to rest.

The grandfather was very drunk and slept like the dead.

The sound of the wolves did not wake him.

Nor did the old man awaken when the young *borracho,* drunk himself, shook him while he snored on. The noise of the creatures somewhere out in the darkness terrified the youngster, who wet his pants and bawled, snot running down his face. The shapes moved in the canyons, huge and hairy, eyes red as coals, fangs like rows of barbed wire in their mouths.

Closing in.

Hector should have taken the gun.

For the rest of his days he blames himself for what happened to his grandfather. The gun was big and heavy but he had fired it before and could have managed it then. How many times had his *abuelo* explained about silver? Why had he not listened?

The hulking forms drew closer in the gloom, growling like rolling thunder and fear got the best of Hector. He was just a little boy.

He hid the only place he could.

Under the cart.

Hector was very small and the transom was low with just enough space for him to squeeze into and hide if he didn't move a muscle or make a sound. So he lay there petrified and listened as the werewolves came. He heard everything. Their paws padding on the ground, then the wood creaking above his head as they stomped onto the carriage, splintering the boards, savage slavering snarls and chomping teeth tearing and rending flesh and the awful meaty wet *crack* and *snap* of his grandfather's limbs being chewed off and devoured. At least the old man never screamed, for he never awoke.

The luck of the drunk.

No such luck for the *nino borracho* who had to listen to the werewolves a foot above him feast on his *abuelo* with lip-smacking relish. And the poor boy could not get away from those sounds under the wagon for he was too afraid to cover his ears, to move or even breathe.

Or cover his nose.

The smell of the werewolf would never be forgotten to him.

Don't move or they will find you and eat you, he warned himself in his mind.

Then, a half-hour later when the last bone was cracked and the last bit of marrow slurped, the creatures departed, their shapes dimly seen through the wooden spokes of the wagon wheels.

They had not eaten him.

Hector would later realize the smell of the whisky in his pores had disguised the scent of his blood so the werewolves did not smell him. From that day forward the *borracho* drank whisky every day of his life.

The sun came up before the little boy ventured forth from his hiding place. All that remained of his beloved grandfather was a few bloody rags and an empty liquor bottle. The child was alone in the vast empty desert and he wanted his mother.

It was on a Sunday when he started back. He knew this because the sound of the church bells led him back to his village.

Now those bells haunt his dreams.

Listen, there they are again.

A faint ringing.

Pulling up the reins of his horse, the old man stops to listen, an hour out of the town he had the silver ammunition made. Sitting in his saddle, surrounded by barren expanse of Durango desertscape on all sides, the *borracho* feels alone in the universe. He hears no bells now, just the whisper of wind in his ears, and knows the bells are a memory from his troubled sleep.

It was a dreadful dream the old man had been having the last month that made him embark on his fateful journey, set him on this path with his silver weapons. An unseen hand is at work and the *borracho* feels a part of some greater plan. For as long as he could remember, the old man had drifted from town to town, flophouse to flophouse, in a drunken blur of alcoholic stupor. He'd begged for money, worked cheap jobs, robbed and stole, paid for his whisky when he could. The *borracho* had waited for death in a ditch somewhere, fully expected it. He wanted to die. That fate became a certainty when the crooked Federales had locked the old man up, before fate and fortune had put him back on the trail re-armed with the dead *policia*'s rifles and pistols and silver. Then came the dream. He has it over and over again, night after night. The vision is so clear and vivid it has to be more than a dream. It is his destiny; a destiny to be fulfilled. It is why, old as he is, broken down as he is, he rides on this horse today alone through the hot badlands, saddlebags laden to overflow with guns and bullets of silver, toward a destination unknown yet always certain.

The old man hears the bells in his sleep.

Sees the church.

And always, the dream is the same.

The church bells ring faint and distant at first, then louder and more insistent until they become deafening, a distorted clanging gong like a sledgehammer on an anvil. All is blackness until the silhouette of the mission steeple appears, impossibly large, against a huge full moon hovering like a yellow and putrid watchful eye. The white adobe walls of the mission are somehow familiar, the bell tower tall and stark against a moon that is always full. Then the church begins to bleed and once it starts bleeding it does not stop. Dark drops of shiny black seep and drip out of the weathered cracks in the façade of the church like tears, until soon the pouring droplets become a flowing gush of bright red blood, hemorrhaging out the pores of the mission, until the walls are white no more, but red wet as fresh paint.

Inside, the screams of infants.

The blood of the innocents.

They are in the church.

As are the werewolves.

The trickster moon lording over them.

The sangre flows like a river, an endless surge of blood bursting in a tidal wave through the church doors and splashing in a great overflowing sea of gore down the hill and this is when he always wakes.

To dream the same dream the next night, and the next, calling him to action.

The old man knows the church. Remembers it as a boy from a place he ages ago abandoned. Understands when he reaches his destination he will find the church and knows what he will find in it.

That is why he has the silver.

Now by instinct he spurs the horse and gallops due northwest, drawing ever closer. The *borracho* needs no map or compass to guide him, for the dream pulls him like a magnet.

Taking him home.

It was high noon, and the village was nowhere in sight.

The bullet hole in Tucker's arm was beginning to hurt something fierce and gave him another reason to be impatient to reach their destination. He needed to wash and bind it before it got inflected. They'd lost time engaging with the Federales and dallying back at the stagecoach junction massacre but it couldn't be helped, though luckily it was hours until sunset. They still had time.

The four riders crossed a plain, flat and unmarred but for the ghost of a mountain range shimmering wetly in the melting waves of heat rising off the desert floor. The three gunfighters and the peasant hadn't said much for the last hour, and none of them had much to discuss. There was the *crunch* of the hooves in the sand and the *clink* of stirrups and *squeak* of leather and not much else. Tucker noticed that Pilar had been preoccupied since the skirmish and refused to meet his eyes now. He wouldn't care but this girl was the key to the silver, and they could ill afford to have her get any second thoughts about taking them to her town. She may have become worried about her people now she'd seen the kind of killers they were. *Women*, he cursed privately, *never just come out and tell you what's on their mind.*

"Spit it out," he said.

The peasant girl finally spoke. "Those Federales were after you. Why? Did you rob a bank?"

"No," stated Bodie flatly.

Fix grunted. "We don't do that."

Pilar looked at her hands clutching her reins. "What crime did you commit that they would offer such a reward?"

Tucker lit a cigarette, his jaw muscles working under the stubble. "Them Federales was dirty."

"I see."

"No. You don't. You ever heard of The Cowboys?"

"*Si. Vaqueros.* Like you."

"No, *The* Cowboys. A gang."

A blank look.

Fix looked over at her from the saddle, and made a finger twirl above his head. "Red sashes?"

Pilar looked down, shrugging in ignorance. "Sorry."

Tucker went on. "Well, we rode with a gang for a few years went by that name. We came regular over the border from Arizona, stole cattle here, drove 'em back into the States. Rustling cattle out of Mexico across into New Mexico and Arizona is big business. Steal it here, sell it there at a discount. Cheap beef."

Pilar nodded, staring straight ahead, trying to understand. "You are rustlers and this is why the Federales wanted you."

Fix sent a projectile of chewing tobacco saliva against a rock where it exploded in a splatter of brown crud. "Wrong, your damn Federales are in on it. They get paid off. Hell, they protected our runs and covered our asses."

Bodie went on. "Last year we did a run, rustled a herd in from Durango, crossed the Rio Grande and got met up by some U.S. Marshals. Our compadres and us was caught red handed and it was a standoff. Guns loaded and drawn. The Cowboys wanted to shoot the Marshals."

Fix snorted. "We shot our compadres instead."

Tucker picked up the tale. "Wasn't going to be part of no lawmen killing. We turned ourselves in, got tried, did a stretch in Yuma, time off for saving the Marshals. But like I said, cattle rustling is big business both sides of the border, and The Cowboys put a price on our head for shooting some of their number. It's mebbe a thousand of them, just three of us, so we hightailed it to Mexico. Been down here ever since."

"Figured we'd hide out," Bodie said.

"Thought we'd be safe," said Fix.

"But The Cowboys got that reward out, and the Federales here are in league with 'em, and that's who those boys were."

Pilar smiled brightly. "So you are not really bad?"

Fix glowered and spoke softly. "Bad enough."

Tucker searched her face, curious. "It don't bother you hiring men like us?"

Pilar held his gaze. "You are dangerous men. My village needs dangerous men to drive away the evil."

That settled, they rode on.

"You was telling us about what happened in your town and what we're riding up against." Tucker adjusted his reins. "Finish your story."

The peasant girl sat in her saddle, and her eyes darkened as she told them the rest. "The second night, The Men Who Walk Like Wolves came . . ."

I remember back to my village that night, and feel the fresh terror in my bones.

Full moon high.

A moon so big like I have never seen. It is like a horrid yellow eye, so huge, a terrible deity watching us, unblinking, full of murder. There is no getting away from it. I see the moon outside when I lock the door and then see it hover in the window when I bolt the wooden shutters and still the bright, horrid light cuts through the slats like fingers feeling through the cracks to seize us. My mother is crying and she prays quietly, clutching her cross. I put my arms around her, and we huddle in our home, but it offers no shelter or protection. We avoid the moonlight and stay in the shadows, as if that would help. The moon casts a light that exposes my people to those who would destroy us, flushes us out of the shadows and gives us nowhere to hide. We pray for sun in vain, for mother moon rules the heavens now, and her terrible children are coming out to play. Those who wait lurking in the hills were born of her, the trickster moon, and the stories of The Men Who Walk Like Wolves have been passed down from fathers to sons in our village long past remembering. You told me they were children's tales, Mama, but how wrong you were. We were fools to think they were legend. Because now they are here.

The terrifying wolflike baying is echoing from out in the hills. But louder and closer than yesterday. It is deafening and hurts my ears, high howling and deep growling, and there are so many. I cover Mama's ears, but know she hears. Please God, strike me deaf so at least I will not have to hear these horrible sounds.

A pounding on the door.

They are here.

No, not them. Rodrigo calling for us to come out. Go back to your hut I cry, but he persists. I go to the door and crack it open and see his sweating face and behind him the town square is full of frightened people. My townsmen have all left their homes and are gathered by the fountain, carrying guns, pitchforks, machetes and torches. The old priest gestures with his arms toward the pueblo church on the hill. He makes a prayer gesture with his hands. We listen to the minister. We will hide in our church where God would surely protect us.

I am among the crowd, the long black tresses of my hair tumbling over my shawled bosom, walking with my mother. Led by the parson, my townspeople march up the hill, eyes fearfully looking out into the darkened hills as we hear the wolf howls. The priest prolongs our lives by bringing the entire village into the church, leading our people in a long procession up the hill through the open wooden doors. But the reverend makes all of the men leave their guns and machetes outside the chapel. There is fear and reluctance in the men's faces, but my people are simple and do as their minister bids. Giving up our guns quickened many of our deaths, but those weapons would not have saved us in the end.

The full moon rears its ugly head.

The priest gathers his flock and against the protests of the more macho farmers, he cajoles and begs and leads his congregation into the chapel.

Now, he bolts the doors with a heavy wood beam.

My people gather in the pews and he takes to the altar and leads our town in prayer. "Oh Heavenly Father we pray . . ."

From outside the stone and wood church, the roars of the wolves shake the night.

We light candles that flicker and gleam on the rows of silver candlesticks and silver plates and silver statues of the Blessed Virgin that adorn the nave. We are a devout congregation, and all extra money of the town has gone into manufacturing these offerings to our Lord.

Look, Pilar, see the eyes of the three gunfighters you have enlisted, how they glint with greed as I tell them of the silver. Soon it will be theirs. Have I done the right thing bringing them to it? I believe they are good men, but that silver is such temptation. I am suddenly full of doubt but Tucker tells me to go on with my story so I continue.

The village kneels and prays, huddling together for safety as we hear the muffled howls outside the walls growing ever louder until the stained-glass windows rattle.

Then all at once the windows explode inward and surging wind from the outside snuffs out the candles.

In the sudden darkness come the man-sized, hairy shapes leaping through the shattering glass, moonlight gleaming on their furry talons, rows of white fangs and red eyes.

The werewolves are too many to count as they fall on us praying villagers, ripping us limb from limb.

The priest is the first to die, his head shorn from his shoulders, rolling over and over down the aisle, spraying blood on the pews. A wolfman sinks its powerful jaws into the pastor's decapitated but still thrashing body, digging into his rib cage and chewing out his beating heart.

Where is Mama? I can't see her.

I scramble through the pews, searching for my mother, ducking the blood and limbs flying through the air and bodies rushing to and fro, many of them already torn and dying. It is pandemonium. Through the broken windows the ghastly glow from the full moon pours onto the nightmare tableau like stage lighting of a play by Satan.

Fangs snap strung with blood and meat.

Red eyes glint in the darkness.

Huge muscled and tailed hairy figures drag my people to the ground and feed.

The women are stripped of their clothes by claws that rake over their nakedness as the werewolves violently ravish the females before eating them.

The massive canine haunches of the beasts pound themselves between the girls' thighs and pulverize their womanhood even as they tear out their throats.

Children are swallowed whole.

The church is bathed in blood and guts during the unspeakable savagery. Screams and roars and rending flesh and bone become a deafening symphony of death echoing in the recesses of our rural church.

I search for Mama, screaming her name, but do not see her.

A handful of peasant men, cowarded by the carnage, abandon their dying wives and children and pry loose the wooden beam that blocks the door, fleeing into the night. They shame me.

The unlucky few who grabbed their rifles and machetes rush back into the church to shoot or hack the werewolves, but soon discover the uselessness of such weaponry against creatures such as these. Those unfortunates swiftly join the dead, dying and devoured.

The others spill through the open doors and run for their lives away from the church and back to the village for their horses. They do not look back but can hear the awful roars and the screams and the ripping of meat and that is enough.

I am among them.

God help me, I am so scared I have abandoned my mother to the mercy of those monsters.

When we reach the stables we find our horses disemboweled, the dead animals submerged in a lake of blackish blood filling the corral. The werewolves knew we would only be able to flee them on foot now, and could not get far.

But when we few look back up the hill to the defiled church, we see the big four-legged shapes up on their haunches watching us, red eyes warning us to stay put.

We stayed put.

This night of blood passed as all nights finally must.

The stables were lit by the rosy threatening glow of the pre-dawn sky.

Just before sunrise the werewolves retreated into Santa Sangre and the church doors were closed. Such was our fear, the surviving townsmen and I remained frozen in place in the stables, some soiling themselves, too afraid to budge.

It was the longest night of our lives. We were afraid to abandon the town and our families and afraid to go back so we just waited, wept and prayed.

The full moon waned. A pale sun rose.

As it did, we heard strange and frightening new sounds come from inside Santa Sangre. Howls of wolves became tortured cries of men, as flesh and bones tore and cracked amidst violent thrashing and thumping noises.

Those of us huddling in the corral had wondered with desperate hope if the werewolves were dying or dead.

By now the sun was full up, and all sounds within Santa Sangre ceased as we stood below in the village watching the too quiet church. Then there was a creak as the doors opened.

The bandits stepped out into broad daylight.

The big men were bearded, long haired, swarthy, scarred and filthy. Their faces and hands were smeared with dried blood and all were naked.

The werewolves had returned to human form. Banditos. They commanded two of the village men to walk one mile southwest and bring them the horses with their clothes they had left there. Two cowering farmers hurried down the hill after receiving the bandits' instructions.

In the corral, I listened on as the fearful men talked amongst themselves. We debated whether to find more rifles and shoot these fiends who now were of human shape. Naked, unarmed and perhaps vulnerable.

As if in reply to the question, we heard the anguished sobs of women that my fellow villagers grimly recognized as the cries of their daughters.

The bandits dragged out five naked young women through the doors of Santa Sangre, their bosoms and buttocks nude and bleeding from scratches, blood streaming down to their feet from between their legs, the result of unimaginable violations. The wolves who now were men clenched the women in front of themselves as body shields, the animalistic fiends grinning sadistically in the hot daylight. The bandits rubbed themselves obscenely against the hindquarters of the girls, and become aroused lapping their tongues in their victims' ears.

The girls' eyes begged their fathers to save and not abandon them, tears flowing down their bloody cheeks, and my townsmen below fell to their knees.

We knew then because they had our wives and daughters and families that we would do the werewolves' bidding now and forever. Whatever that may be.

So as the day moved on, I stood alone in my hut, watching a group of browbeaten villagers carrying supplies up the hill under the baking sun toward the bandits waiting by the church.

For the next four weeks after the bandits had taken and occupied the church they now called Santa Sangre, they enslaved my people.

We brought the bandits food, clothes and drink.

When the food ran out, one brave but foolish man, Pablo, had offered his life for his daughter and walked up the long hill through the front doors of the church and was never seen again.

You have their attention, Pilar. These gunslingers' eyes are wide as saucers as they hear my story. The day is hot as we ride our tired horses through the noon sun burning down, but I swear I see them shiver as if chilled. My town is close now. I recognize the hills. Do these hard men believe me? I think they are at least respectful of what they have come to fight, and they will see with their own eyes soon enough, soon enough. There, I see the distant steeple of the church, a gleam of metal off the bell. We are almost there. I must finish my tale.

When my hut was quiet in the still of the night, I lay awake and wept and listened to the sobbing of my people from the chapel below the shadowed steeple of Santa Sangre. The moon grew fuller night by night. I knew that it would be a full moon once again in two, maybe three days, and The Men Who Walk Like Wolves would eat the last of us. I knew what I had to do.

I sat by my mirror, took a set of scissors and began shearing my long black hair. It was my pride, and I watch sadly as the locks fall to the floor. I make faces in the glass, practicing to look like a man, not a girl, because vaqueros dangerous enough to kill the things that came to our town would not listen to a woman. Well, would you have, Señors? I thought not. I dressed in a poncho and pants I took from my neighbor's house who was dead and would not need them. The worst part was when I had to steal a horse because it meant climbing the hill to the church and getting close to the sleeping bandits, but luck was with me because the moon was clouded and it was very dark and none of the bandits stirred when I untied the horse from the post behind the cathedral without a sound.

Today I left to find a few brave gunfighters who would help us rout this scourge. I had already named them.

They would be The Guns of Santa Sangre.

CHAPTER SEVEN

THEY REACHED SANTA SANGRE BY NOON, THE FOUR riding onto the ridge overlooking the village.

The sun beat down directly overhead.

Tucker eyeballed the peasant. "Stay put."

The cowboys drew their irons, dropped from their saddles onto the dirt into a low crouch and moved swiftly to the edge of the embankment to survey the scene and get the lay of the land. Peering over the edge, the gunfighters scoped out the town down in the valley below.

It was just as the girl described it. The village consisted of twenty or so wooden huts with straw and plank roofs situated in a dusty basin about five hundred yards wide between three hills leading out to the desert. There was a large fountain with a cement pinnacle rising out of the brackish water in the center of the square. A few corrals and stables, now empty, sat amidst the jumble of huts. Several outhouse shacks were visible on the edge of the village.

The church itself sat atop the tallest of the hills to the west, three hundred yards opposite them. It was constructed of white pueblo, granite stones rimming the arch of the two twenty-foot-high wooden doors. A whitewashed steeple jutted toward the sky, the cast iron mission bell visible in the opening below the large cross at its pinnacle.

The chapel led back fifty yards, with two broken stained-glass windows of green and red and purple glass visible on the side facing them. From where the gunfighters crouched, around the other side of the church they could see the shadows of a dozen or more horses on the dirt and rubble of the ridge, tails swishing, tethered to an unseen post.

The large oaken doors of the church were wide open.

There was no wind. The rank air reeked of death and decay.

Tucker took the measure of what he figured would become the battlefield for the fight ahead.

Down on the desolate streets of the town, a few figures on horseback trotted and milled amidst a bunch of scraggly chickens. The cowboys squinted in the sun to make the interlopers out. The bandits were clearly men, not wolves, although they were hairy and feral enough, with beards and long hair. Their clothes were baggy and loose fitting, and they carried many guns with rifles slung over their shoulders and pistols hanging out of holsters on leather belts. Some wore sombreros, some didn't. All were barefoot in their stirrups. No villagers were in plain sight.

Up on the ridge, Tucker looked at his fellow gunmen, scratching his beard. "Those look like ordinary men to me."

Bodie surveyed the area, fingering his Sharps rifle.

"I make out about twenty horses tied to the back of that church," Fix tautly observed. "The rest of them sons of bitches must be in the mission. We're gonna need to get past them to get the silver out of there."

"What's our move?" Bodie asked.

Fix looked to Tucker as they usually did.

"Let's ride down and take out the bandits in the town. Their friends will have to come through the church door to get us, n' if we dig in we can pick 'em off as they come out."

"We have the high ground right here," Fix said. "We could pick off them sumbitches below and still be in good position to get the rest when they come out of the church."

"We only get clean shots at a few in the village from here, and there may be more we can't spot. Plus, the church is too far. We're a little out of range to make our shots count."

"Yeah, you're right. Best ride down and get 'em in our killing field."

The easygoing Swede shrugged. "Sounds as good a plan as any."

Tucker smiled at his friends. "Just think, a few hours ago this morning we were dead broke wondering what to do with ourselves, and now we're all a few bullets shy from being rich men."

"You're forgettin' two things." Fix chewed his plug and spat.

"Which are?"

"First we may all get our asses shot off."

"What's the other?"

"Bitch may be lying and there may be no silver."

"One way to find out."

Fix grinned. The gunfighters moved away from the embankment in a crouch, keeping their heads down so they wouldn't be spotted. They rose when they reached their horses tethered out of sight a safe distance away, grabbed their saddle horns and swung back up in their mounts. Tucker drew his repeater rifle out of his saddle holster and checked it. "Everybody loaded and locked down?"

"Check," said Fix, cocking the Winchester Model 12 pump shotgun in his wiry hands.

"I'm good." Bodie smiled, pinwheeling the two Remington pistols around his forefingers, spinning the guns back into his sideholsters.

"Let's go amongst 'em." Tucker nodded, reining his horse around and starting for the trail leading down the hill into the village. "We got some killin' to do."

Pilar rode up, blocking their way. "No. Wait," she said. "I have something I must show you first. Ride this way." Tucker, Fix and Bodie regarded one another and shrugged, then trotted off after the departing Mexican. The peasant rode with them a short distance down an arroyo on the near side of the ridge. The path wound through granite boulders and green verdant patches of mesquite. Tucker smelled water and saw sunlight glint off a nearby creek through the breaks in the rocks.

The trail spilled out at a small brick building of the local blacksmith's shop. It was deserted. Wooden beams and planks formed a roof over the square bunker of a structure that was covered with char. A large blacked steel chimney rose from the center, but there was no smoke. Inside the large opening on the wall they could see the shadows of metal-making equipment. Cords of firewood were piled behind the rear wall.

The cowboys sat in their saddles as the peasant girl went inside. She gestured for them to follow, so they dismounted. Tucker was antsy, ready for action, and he resented the delay. Right now, the bandits were in the church and only a few were in the town, and the time was right to strike. In a few minutes, many more might be outside and the odds might no longer be stacked in their favor. One glance at his fellow gunfighters' expressions showed him they felt the same. "It's her dime," he grumbled sideways to the other two. They stepped under the straw awning and stood amid the sledgehammers, anvils, kilns and chains littering the dirt floor of the shed. Pilar was gesturing at the implements. "When you get the silver, *señors*, you must bring it here and we will melt it down to make the bullets." The beautiful girl showed them a bullet-making press beside the big cast iron pot placed on a rack for heating over a wooden fire.

"Yeah, sure, right," Fix said.

The gunslingers skulked under the overhang and threw one another bemused glances, humoring the peasant, because none of the three cowboys believed the story about wolfmen or the silver bullets required to kill them. They just wanted to shoot their way past the bandits, grab the silver, get in and get out. But the girl had something else in mind. "You are wounded, *señor*, in the arm. I have medical supplies."

Tucker accepted the bandages, needle and thread that Pilar handed him. "It ain't serious," he mumbled, but went to work treating the wound.

The girl was not through. "You must all be very hungry. *Comida*. We have many hours until sundown and you should have something to eat before your great battle ahead."

Tucker's stomach grumbled. The female made sense. He had not eaten that day and neither had the rest and they could get pinned down for hours trading fire with the bandits if things went south, and that was activity not best engaged on an empty stomach. A little food, then to work directly.

"Wouldn't say no to no grub," Bodie said.

"A man fights better on a full stomach," agreed Fix.

"Thanks, ma'am," Tucker nodded. "Bein' as how many of them sumbitches is out there this meal could be our last."

"Rest your *caballos*. I will cook for you."

The cowboys went outside and tied their horses to the hitching post. They stretched their legs and came back inside the blacksmith's shop, getting out of the brutally beating sun. They passed a bottle of whisky. Pilar built a fire under the kettle. She went to a wooden storage box and brought out cut pieces of a freshly slaughtered chicken, potatoes and carrots, already chopped, and put some ingredients in the pot. Then she poured it full of water from a bucket, adding a fistful of spices from canisters in the box. While the stew heated, she brought the men a loaf of bread and a jug of water out of a closet. The gunfighters dug in as she cooked.

"Lucky for us you had some chow handy," Tucker offered, covering his mouth politely as he talked and ate.

The girl smiled knowingly. "I had gathered provisions for you last night before I rode out. I knew the men I found, I prayed to find, would be hungry when they got to the village and would need their strength."

"It's good to be prepared."

"*Sí.*" As Pilar kneeled by the pot, all of them were watching her ass.

"*Señors*, now you have seen the church. How will you get the silver out of there?"

"Shoot our way out if we have to," Tucker replied.

"Your bullets will not kill them. Remember this."

"If we put them in the right place they will," Fix mused dryly. Tucker and Fix chuckled with him.

That made the girl whirl around in alarm. "You must heed me! The Men Who Walk Like Wolves are not harmed by regular bullets, only silver! I have seen this with my own eyes! This is why you must get the silver and bring it here! Only then when we melt it down—"

"—into silver bullets we can shoot into the heart of the werewolf," Tucker interrupted her. "Yeah, yeah I know, ma'am. You told us about twenty times on the ride. We'll get the silver. You best believe that. Don't worry your pretty head."

"I trust you." She smiled and the simple hope and belief in her eyes made Tucker feel bad.

"I know you do," he replied regretfully.

The blacksmith's shop filled with smoke. The shootists ate their plates of chow quietly, weapons beside them.

By the time they looked up, the girl had left.

☾

The little girl woke.

She had been sleeping with her mother's arms cradled around her. While those aged arms tried to be gentle, they held her like a vise. The child's name was Bonita and she was eight. Her shiny black hair, so much like her sister's, tumbled down her brown angelic face, bleary from sleep. She had hoped when she awoke she would be back in her bed in the hut and none of this had happened, but Bonita saw all the haggard, starving, terrified faces of the villagers and knew that her nightmare was real.

They were in the back room of the church, stockaded like animals.

Where was her sister Pilar, Bonita wondered, why had she not come?

She will, the child repeatedly assured herself.

Pilar had told her she would.

On that terrifying first night when the monsters came, her big sister had grabbed her and carried her to safety in the church as everywhere the monsters were tearing apart the people from the town. Thankfully, Bonita saw nothing. Pilar had clamped her hands over her tiny eyes saying *don't look child* but the little girl could hear and that frightened her badly. The hideous sounds of the man wolves' terrible roars and people screaming and the wet ripping created pictures in her mind that were bad enough. She felt herself gripped tightly against her big sister's large soft bosom and they were moving swiftly and then there was the slam of a door and things quieted and Pilar whispered she could open her eyes. They were in a room and it was very dark but in the moonlight her sister's face hovered above her own, wet with tears of fear and trying to be brave as she stroked her sibling's hair tenderly.

"You must hide here and not come out, *comprende*?"

Bonita, who always did what Pilar said, had nodded.

"Do not make a sound, not matter what."

"I won't."

"I must go."

"No!"

Bonita had wept and begged and hugged Pilar but her older sister sobbed and gently pried her small fingers from their desperate grip on her shoulders.

"Listen to me, *nina*. I promise I will come back for you. I will never leave you but I must go and get help, then come back for you. I need you to be brave. Can you do that?"

Her big sister was everything to the child. Always, the little girl looked up to her, tried to dress like her, behave like her, be good like her and Bonita would always do what Pilar said to do. She promised to be brave and to hide until Pilar returned. Then her older sibling gave her a loving, urgent hug and closed the closet door.

She had not seen her since.

When the fear came, as it did more and more lately, Bonita told herself that Pilar always kept her promises. She would return. And everything would be well.

The child had not been able to hide for long. The next day the monsters were gone but there were horrible men in their place. They threw the villagers into the back room of the church and used it as a place to hold them. Bonita was discovered in the closet immediately. *It was not my fault* she would tell her sister when she came, because she would never want Pilar to think she had broken a promise.

Her stomach ached with hunger.

Against the walls, the other villagers sat, knees drawn up, heads down. Their faces were emaciated and haggard and their eyes were black holes from the diet of fear they lived on. Nobody spoke, not anymore. Their number grew less every few days as the hairy men would come in and grab one at random; dragged out kicking, begging, weeping, that villager would not be seen again. Bonita would pray it was not her turn and cover her ears against the screaming she would hear behind the door—but thankfully the cries did not last long.

Pilar would come.

She never lied.

The room stank with the odor of people who had not bathed in a month. The closet she had hid in weeks before had been turned into a latrine with a slop bucket inside where they would go to relieve themselves. This became less frequent because the bad men barely fed them. Crusts of bread and water and a few pieces of slaughtered pigs from the village were tossed in once in a while. Swarms of flies buzzed around the smelly closed door.

Bonita huddled in her mother's arms but those arms had grown steadily weaker over the passing days. When she looked in her parent's face she saw a pale tight mask lined with pain and terror. For the first weeks, her mother had prayed softly and brushed the little girl's hair over and over, but lately those prayers had stopped and Bonita's hair grew tangled and unkempt. It fell to the child who was holding onto her mother to comfort her parent, not the other way around.

My sister will come, don't cry, Mama.

She promised.

And promises are to be kept.

A child's faith sustained her because for her it was a simple fact.

The bolt on the outside of the storeroom door rattled and slammed aside.

Bonita's guts clenched.

The door swung open and one of the hairy men stood there, sniffing and glowering like an animal. He had come for one of them. The people cringed as his black eyes swung over them, back and forth.

Settling on Bonita.

It was her turn, she knew.

He would take her from the room never to return.

Hurry, Pilar.

The bandit's boots creaked on the old floorboards as he walked over and towered above her. Bonita felt her mother's arms tighten but they were parchment thin and had no strength.

The little boy Raul who sat beside her looked at her face so she said goodbye to him with her eyes.

The hairy one suddenly reached down with a filthy hand, grabbing hair. The boy's, not hers. Raul shrieked as he was lifted up by the head off the ground and carried like a chicken out the door with the bandit.

The door slammed closed and the bolt was thrown and Bonita covered her ears to the terrible high-pitched screaming, but as usual it did not last long.

Pilar had never felt so filthy. She had ridden for ten hours in the hot sun and dust and was coated with disgusting layers of sweat and caked with the grime and the mud she had smeared all over herself for a disguise. She stank. The girl felt like a rotten vegetable and not even like a woman. She was strong of heart, had braved much the last day, but she was also female and her dirtiness buried her self-esteem. She could bear it no longer.

The deep creek lay ahead.

In her mind, she could already feel the cold, refreshing waters on her skin. It would only take five minutes. The men were eating, behind her in the shed, and would not discover her if she bathed fast. The girl threw a cautious glance over her shoulder and saw nobody had followed her. She was alone. Reaching the edge of the waters, she disrobed quickly behind a big rock, pulling her baggy shirt over her head and when she loosened the wrapped cloth over her bosom, her heavy breasts tumbled out. Stepping out of her pants, she tossed the foul-smelling discarded clothes into a heap behind the rock, and walked stark naked in the waist-deep water with a shuddering gasp of relief. Her flesh tingled as she dunked her head beneath the rippling surface, hair soaked, re-emerging and spitting water. The rush of the current felt good and cold against her breasts, and her big brown nipples crinkled like little pebbles. She scrubbed hard. Everywhere. With a desperate exhilaration, she used her hands to cleanse her face, her armpits, her stomach, the thick bristle between her legs and her buttocks, washing herself top to bottom. Soon her skin felt smooth, supple and voluptuous again. Pilar began to feel renewed, a flesh and blood girl once more, and the simple act of getting washed up cleared her mind and removed her dread along with the accumulated dirt. She stood up on the slippery rocks in water just above her knees and splashed herself with the creek runoff, shaking her head as her sopping hair smacked her neck. The dry desert heat felt good on her breasts and thighs, drying the warming cold water dripping down her naked body. She could stand here forever.

And that is when she saw him.

The giant they called Bodie.

Pilar's rump had been turned to the trail back to the blacksmith's shop and she had not seen or heard him come down. Now there he was just standing on the bank with the big fool lopsided grin on his lantern jaw, his eyes ogling her with unbridled lust. With a startled cry, Pilar crossed her arms over her exposed chest and covered her privates, turning her backside away from him, bent down in embarrassment to disguise her nudity—but he could see everything. To make matters worse, the girl slipped and lost her balance, taking her arms away from her body as she clambered up, so he saw her nude all over again. And that was when she saw the place where she had dropped her garments was empty. He was holding her clothes with a dirty smirk. She faced him and stood bare-assed and dripping. Her beautiful brown eyes flashed in alarm but she held the grinning cowboy's gaze while he eyeballed her boldly up and down.

"*Por favor*," she whispered.

He unbuckled his trousers.

She struggled to keep looking at his eyes.

He teasingly held the clothes out for her a few feet away and she had no choice but to remove her hand from her bosom.

"You shore are purty," Bodie said.

This was it.

He would take her.

They would all take her.

Maybe at least they would kill the werewolves when they were finished.

"Bodie!" Tucker barked. Both Pilar and Bodie turned to see Tucker and Fix sitting on their horses, armed and ready to go. They had the Swede's horse with them.

"Shit," Bodie said.

"We got work," said the leader.

"Man needs a little relaxation," mumbled the giant cowboy.

"Mount up."

"I was about to."

"Your horse, idiot."

With a petulant scowl of disappointment, Bodie tossed Pilar her clothes. He heaved a huge sigh, turned and stomped up the trail like a big baby to where his comrades sat on their horses. The girl quickly ducked behind a boulder on the shore and got dressed. The Swede swung into the saddle of his horse, buttoning his fly as they headed back up the trail. Tugging on her drawers and slipping her feet into her sandals, still dripping wet, the peasant girl took off in a run to catch up with the gunslingers before they rode down into the village. She got to the top of the arroyo back at the blacksmith's shop right as the three riders were turning their horses around to shove off up the trail.

In the gap, Tucker reined his stallion around and blocked the Mexican from getting back on her horse. "Wait for us here and when we get the silver we'll come back." His eyes were hard but she guessed he was just looking out for her. This was the dangerous business of killing and was the whole reason she had brought professionals of their fearsome trade to this place. She knew nothing of gunplay, and he was right, she would just get in the way and what good would she be to her mother and sister dead.

"Good luck," was all she said.

The peasant watched them ride out, her face bright with pure hope and faith.

Backs to her in their saddles, out of earshot of the girl behind them, the hard men shared a smirk.

"Good luck is right, because none of us got any intention of coming back," Fix murmured.

"If or when we get any silver, we be long gone," Bodie said.

"We got to get the silver first," Tucker pointed out.

"That's a fact," said Fix.

The sun was high and brutally hot as the men rode up. The trail passed by the embankment where they had scouted the town, then widened as it turned into a downgrade leading to the western edge of the village. The three rode slow, their weapons close at hand, the only sounds the clop of hooves, occasional snort of their horses, tumble of dislodged stones and the squeak of saddle leather. They were on full alert, their eyes moving left and right in a clockwork scan. The time for killing had come, and this was what they were good at and all talk ceased, because as the adrenaline began to pump and their senses became sharp, the three were one. Gradually, the trail spilled out at the base of the valley and put them eye level with the first shacks of the place they had come to clean up.

The village lay ahead.

The gunfighters rode fearlessly down into the town and past the adobe huts and wood fence corrals of the settlement that was quiet as a cemetery. It was preternaturally silent. The three rode side by side in a flank formation. Then they saw movement. Five bandits rode their horses around the area, eyeballing them. The big hairy men in the loose-fitting clothes and cut-off vests were armed to the teeth in their dusty weathered saddles, their open shirts showing the coarse black hair on their unwashed chests. Swarming flies buzzed around them. Their horses seemed cowed and fearful of their owners, eyes wide with fear. Tucker, Bodie and Fix just kept riding, like nothing was happening. Five more bandits appeared as if out of nowhere. Now there were ten. The gunfighters rode on through the town, hands near their pistols and rifles, waiting for the banditos to make a move, but the slimy brigands just watched them curiously, and assembled. Tucker had seen enough wolves in his life to admit to himself these scum shared the same wary, head bobbing, unblinking way of regarding a man.

Bodie chuckled. "Wolves who walk like men, my ass. These are just plain old bandits, boys. But I can see how the villagers might've gotten that impression bein' as these varmints are mangier than any coyotes I can recall."

Fix clicked his teeth. "We don't need to waste the silver on bullets, that'd be too good for 'em."

Tucker's gaze moved left and right. "There's sure a lot of 'em."

Then all of a sudden the Jefe was right in front of them, straddling his horse and blocking their way. He was a huge, fat Mexican man of indeterminate age with long hair streaked with gray and ammunition belts crisscrossing his chest. He looked very strong despite his girth.

"What are you doing, here, *Señors?*" He spoke in a gravelly sing song voice, grinning wide to reveal a full mouthful of gold teeth glinting in the sun.

"Just riding through," Tucker said.

"You can ride lots of places, yet you are here," said the Mexican.

"It's a place as good as any."

Tucker held the Jefe's visceral gaze. Another bandito rode up. This one held himself to his saddle with just his powerful knees, because his hands were occupied gripping the naked ass of a nude village girl facing him in the saddle, his hands pumping her buttocks slowly and deeply up and down on his hips. He was not wearing pants. The unclad girl submitted passively to her rape, her body lacerated with bleeding cuts, sores and bruises from being scratched and chewed. Her bare breasts draped against his chest, arms hung at her sides, head limp on his shoulder, eyes wide and glazed, brutalized past caring.

Tucker, Bodie and Fix watched the spectacle in disgust, the true horror of the situation sinking in.

The bandit eyeballed them with a drooling grin as he finished with the girl, holding fistfuls of her bare butt, slapping her hips onto his harder and harder as he started to grunt. His thighs tightened, and veins in his neck bulged as he roared with release.

The gunfighters stared on in utter mortification, fingers tickling the stocks of their holstered pistols.

Holding their gaze lasciviously, the bandit slowly smiled, getting hard again inside the girl. Holding her limp thighs, he started humping her in the saddle slowly and lustfully all over again. He might as well have been screwing a corpse.

The three gunslingers regarded one another with cold murder.

The Jefe grinned at them with a wide mouth of gold teeth. "Come with us, amigos. Drink. Be friendly." He smelled like a dog. The cowboys wrinkled their nose at his stench. "I am Mosca. These are my men. This is Calderon. He is my second."

Tucker kept his eyes on the bandits who now surrounded them on all sides, tightening his horse up next to Fix and Bodie's saddles. Leaning in, he scratched his nose and whispered, "I savvy we get inside that church, see if that silver is there at all and this ain't no big goose chase."

His companions nodded slowly.

Tucker looked at Mosca and tipped his hat. "Lead the way."

The Jefe grinned, and spurred his horse. "Follow me."

So the three gunfighters urged their horses and followed, escorted by Mosca and Calderon in the lead and the nine bandits to their rear. Tucker knew they were handily flanked fore and aft, but they had to play it out. As they trod through the square of the besieged village, the cowboy looked left and right at the eerily deserted huts and shacks. It had the stink and ennui of a graveyard. Give up hope all ye who enter here. Vultures were everywhere, the foul carrion birds strolling to and fro unchallenged down the streets and byways of the empty town like they owned the place, the true citizens of the village now. The buzzards picked at pieces of flesh and bloody shags of meat that they happened upon. They didn't fight over them as such scavenger birds usually did, because there was plenty of meat to be found. In the sky overhead, a dozen vultures circled in constant circumference, their shadows falling over the men's hats.

The seconds ticked by into minutes as the group rode patiently through town, to the metronome beat of the horses' hooves.

Tucker looked ahead past the heads of the two brigands. Down the dirt street, the cowboy saw the stark white pueblo church looming above on the hill, a place of iniquity drawing closer like inescapable destiny. Vultures perched on the steeple and rooftops of the mission congregated like crows on telegraph wires, from this distance resembling rows of black teeth against the blinding whitewash of the adobe structure. They were in there, the villagers that were left, and his stomach clenched in dread anticipating what they would witness inside the church minutes from now. It was going to be bad. He remembered too well the horrors of the stagecoach junction massacre they had come upon earlier that morning, and this would be worse. But the silver was in there. All they had to do was get it and somehow get out.

Perhaps the bandits meant to kill them once they had passed the open wooden doors of the mission that beckoned like a gaping mouth up on the ridge, but somehow Tucker doubted that was the plan. Mosca and his men could easily have opened fire on them right here down in the square. Looking over his shoulder, he saw the hairy Mexican banditos riding patently behind, making no move for their many guns, though their present position gave them the perfect opportunity to shoot the gunslingers in the back.

The one ahead on the right called Calderon looked back at Tucker and winked, the up and down movement of the horse doing his work for him as he pleasured himself inside the half-dead meat puppet of the girl in his lap, her arms thrown limply over his shoulders in a grotesque mockery of a lover's embrace. The bandit was a lean, feral vulpine man with a long snout of nose who bore a natural resemblance to a rabid coyote. Tucker broke his dull, ugly gaze and stole laconic glances left and right to Bodie and Fix. His confederates were staring straight ahead at the mission they called Santa Sangre, braced for battle, hands on their pistols. Like it or not, they were all about to find out why it was now called Saint Blood.

The gunfighters trotted with the bandits up the paved hill to the pueblo church of Santa Sangre. The heat seemed to get hotter the higher they ascended. The upgrade was a wide gravel path that rose farther and farther above the opposite embankment, and the cluttered sprawl of village huts shrank below as the shadow of the steeple fell over them.

A broad ridge about fifty yards wide formed a natural perimeter around the religious structure. The ground was rock and dirt, and they all rode around the back of the church. They dismounted and tethered their horses on the rail in the shade behind the cathedral. About twenty other horses, saddles and bridles were tied to the same hitching post.

The cowboys exchanged glances, now having a good idea of the actual number of the opposing forces. The three had the bullets, if they had the luck.

Tucker saw the early afternoon sun moving down the sky in the direction of the distant Durango Mountains. He whispered to his comrades. "Savvy we got five hours till nightfall and the full moon."

The stark sunlight was blinding and bleached the outside of the church blank white, but inside the open oaken doors the interior of the cathedral was pitch black. The bandits stood back to allow their guests to enter the doorway.

When the three gunfighters set foot inside the church, the stench nearly pitched them backward. It was the disgusting, gorge-rising odor of dead meat, rot and death in the stifling enclosed quarters. Tucker, Bodie and Fix stepped into the nave with utter revulsion. Their spurs jingled, ringing through the catacombs of Santa Sangre. Diffused light filtered through the broken stained-glass windows into an area more animal cave than chapel. The silhouettes of more than a dozen bandits hunkered and sprawled in the pews. Some chewed on bones. Others played cards. Still others slept curled up like dogs, snoring loudly. One of them urinated against a far wall. Sunlight glinted on the dull metal of guns, blades of knives and machetes.

Tucker's eyes grew accustomed to the darkness.

Chunks of human meat and flesh, both fresh and decayed, were piled everywhere on the tiles. Bones and skulls, gnawed clean, had been heaped waist high. The blood pooling on the floor was shiny and wet or black as dried paint. Flies swarmed in a steady maddening drone. Gore dripped. In one corner of the defiled abattoir of the church once known as Santa Tomas, several naked young women sat cowering in the darkness, hugging their knees. They shivered, bruised and limp, eyes dead, too broken to care as they waited to be used at the whim of the bandits.

"Lordy," whispered Tucker.

"Where are the rest of the villagers?" Bodie wondered.

"Reckon they're that wet stuff your boots is standing in," Fix observed grimly, nodding at the huddled group of bare, savaged girls. "They all that's left, what's left of 'em."

In the murky darkness, shiny things gleamed. The shimmering came from glinting metal objects placed all around the room. It was silver. Statues. Candlesticks. Plates. The precious metal shined regal and bright in the cathedral, and the reflections flashed in the eyes of the three gunfighters.

What they had come for.

The blasting light from the sun through the doorway behind them silhouetted the three cowboys and cast their shadows thirty feet ahead down the aisle as they walked tall through the grisly pews. The gunslingers' eyes were riveted on the silver treasures before them. Their lips parted and drew breath at the riches they beheld. The shiny beams danced on their faces, and they forgot the unspeakable horror all around them as they approached the altar, hypnotized by the glory of the silver, more than they could have dreamed. The treasure was actual. Tucker saw the wonder in Fix and Bodie's eyes, silver reflected light rippling on their faces in liquid refraction, like the sun off a river. A man would never have an opportunity like this again. The gunfighter wanted rid of this place. He felt hatred for the bandits and outrage for the people, but he was not responsible for their fate. This was more money than he could ever spend. *Forget the stench, put it out of your mind*, he told himself. *Don't look at those young girls, you can't do nothing for them. It will be all over for them soon, anyway. Keep your mind on the silver. Don't listen to their wails and sobbing, people suffer in this world. You didn't put them here.*

But you can get them out, a stubborn voice in his head told him as he forced it into the back of his conscience, telling himself he had to get the three of them out first. He had one big problem, and as he exchanged glances with his fellow gunsels, he saw they were thinking the same damn thing.

How the hell were they going to get the silver out of there?

Well those stinking scum damn sure weren't going to just let them walk out with it. Tucker automatically gauged the killing ground and did some fast calculations in his head. The others were doing the same. The three gunfighters communicated wordlessly by directional eye movements and subtle hand signals to work out the strategy of the pending shoot-out that could be seconds away. Most of the bandits now appeared to be behind them, near the front of the church. A finger point and open palm gesture by Fix. There were but two of the animals loitering behind the tabernacle they had to worry about and the gunslingers would pick them off first. Tucker nudged his chin. There were about fourteen pews, which would afford them ample cover and shield them from the bullets. Bodie and Fix imperceptively nodded. An eye movement from Bodie. The naked girls in the corner would be directly in the line of fire. Tucker didn't like that, but they did not have time to get them out of harm's way, didn't have time, period. Fix reached up to scratch his nose and drew his thumb across his throat. Tucker felt terrible, those poor girls who had suffered so much were dead meat when the bullets flew. He tried to tell himself they were just being put out of their misery. *Keep your mind on the silver, and at least you'll be killing those bastards for them.*

Then the silver was suddenly swallowed in shadow when a wall of blackness descended as the big oaken doors were slammed shut behind them with a resounding *boom*.

The gunfighters turned, hands by their guns.

The Jefe and the bandits stood at the other end of the pew by the closed doors with their arms crossed. On both sides, the other bandits, acting drunk or sleepy, were rising from their spoor to regard their new visitors. It seemed they were salivating. Mosca grinned, flashing rows of gold teeth, and spread his arms wide in generosity and welcome. "*Mi casa es su casa.*"

Tucker spat. "You're a real nice bunch of guys."

Mosca winked. "Stay and party with us. Have a drink. You want a woman?"

Bodie winced at the sight of the brutalized females. "We'll pass." Some of the bandits standing nearby were sniffing the scent of the gunslingers. Fix shot one of them a look that made them retreat fast.

The Jefe spoke softly. "I ask you again, amigos, what have you come here for?"

Tucker looked at Bodie and Fix, then looked at the bandit leader and came right out with it. "Silver."

The bandit leader walked down the aisle of the nave between the pews, nodding, eyeing the treasures of the tabernacle. "*Si. Entiendo.* Much silver. *Mucho dinero.* You want this, *si*?"

"Yup."

"Then take it." Mosca shrugged affably. "It is yours."

Tucker kept his hands near his pistols. They were outnumbered ten to one. "Just like that?" he said.

"*Si*, just like that. Take it and go."

The gunslingers exchanged glances.

"Thanks," said Bodie.

"With our regards." With a wave of his arm, Mosca gestured for his men to open the front doors of the church. "*Hombres*, fetch the saddlebags of the *caballeros* so they may take the silver." A group of bandits lifted the beam and the oaken doors swung wide, blasting daylight into the church, as they went outside. The Jefe just stood with his arms crossed, presiding over the slaughterhouse of a defiled cathedral scattered with piles of human remains, bones and drying blood that festooned the walls, floors and pews.

"What's the catch?" asked Tucker.

Mosca shrugged. "We have no use of silver."

"So we heard," Fix quipped.

The Jefe chuckled. "Or gold. Or *dinero*. Men like us, we take what we want. Nobody stops us. What need have we of *dinero*?" The bandito walked up to Tucker, seeming to sniff him. His breath was foul and canine, steaming in the air, but his eyes were powerful and primal as a wild coyote and owned the gunslinger's gaze with the respect of the strong. "You have killed many men, *si*?"

"Reckon."

"And you. And you." Mosca nodded at Bodie, and then at Fix. "I see this. You are cruel men, yes, and strong. *Muy gusta.* So I make you this proposition. Ride with us."

The gunfighters exchanged laconic glances.

"Join us," spoke the Jefe.

The leader of the gunfighters spoke for all three. "Thanks, but we ride alone."

"Lone wolves, eh?"

"Something like that."

The bandit leader threw his head back and laughed. His men laughed. It was contagious. Even the gunslingers joined in and laughed.

"Lone wolves." Mosca gave an old, knowing smile. "We know about wolves, amigos, and because of this I tell you it is true what they say. Lone wolves are easy targets."

"We'll take our chances." Fix's jaw slowly worked on a chaw of tobacco, measured and deliberate.

"Join us, amigos! You will never be alone. And you will live forever. Be free. But the choice is yours." Three bandits came back through the open doors of Santa Sangre carrying the gunfighters' saddlebags, and dropped them at the floor of their owners' feet. "Your silver." The Jefe gestured to the tabernacle. "Take it all."

Wary and incredulous, Tucker, Bodie and Fix eyed one another and the bandits. The offer seemed good. With one hand near a gun, each one of the gunfighters began using the other hand to grab the candlesticks and stuff them in their saddlebags. They whispered to one another out of earshot of their hosts.

"This is too easy," said Fix.

"What's the catch?" said Bodie.

"It's got to be a trick. They're screwing with us," the other replied.

"Let's take it one step at a time," said Tucker. "First get the silver. Then worry about getting out the door."

Fix almost grinned, tobacco juice on his bad teeth. "We're rich, boys."

"If we live to spend it," observed Bodie.

"Reckon," Tucker added.

When they had taken all of the candlesticks, they greedily grabbed the shining silver platters, their adrenaline beginning to pump. Nobody stood in their way. No one interfered. The chapel was silent save for the clinking of the metal they removed and the quiet mewling of the lost girls in the corner. Their saddlebags were nearly full and brimming with silver before the cowboys got to the back of the alter and lifted the two silver statues of the Virgin Mary.

Then they heard the sobbing.

Tucker looked at Fix, who looked at Bodie, and they put down the precious statues and walked to the small room in back of the tabernacle. There was a wooden door and that door had a small slot. When they opened the panel, through the hole they saw the fifteen surviving villagers of the town locked in the room. The starving people were still alive, just barely, but badly beaten, held captive and imprisoned in the back of the church.

"Damn," whispered Tucker.

"You said it," said Bodie.

"Those sons of bitches. They're gonna eat those people," choked Fix.

Crammed in the small back room of the church like human cattle in a stockade, the peasants saw the hard-sympathetic faces of the shaken gunmen through the slot in the door. They fell to their knees begging and pleading pathetically for help in their native tongue. The unfortunates' eyes were horror holes. "Please . . . please . . . please . . . Help us . . . Save us." The gunfighters heard the words over and over, unable to tear their gaze from the miserable wretches and the three briefly forgot about the silver.

A voice behind them broke the spell. "Forget about them. Those are not men. They are sheep. They are the weak. We are the strong. The strong eat the weak, as wolves eat sheep." Mosca shut the slot on the door. "You three are strong. You must join us. Here you belong, amigos. With us."

The gunfighters turned to face the Jefe. Tucker spoke first. "What's going to happen to them?"

"What happens to all sheep, amigos . . . the slaughter." Mosca's reply was cold and heartless.

Fix bristled. "Those aren't sheep. Them's people. You have every-thing they own. That's enough. Let 'em go."

"Join us or take the silver and go, amigos, before I change my mind." A malignant threat entered the tone of the pitiless bandit leader's voice as his grin became strained and tense, disgusted by the cowboys' empathy he clearly took for a sign of weakness.

The gunfighters regarded one another. They had seen all manner of human cruelty wherever they rode but had never come across the raw savagery that lay before them in Santa Sangre. It stirred a buried humanity deep in their hardened hearts. In their minds were branded the faces of the captive villagers behind the door and the gruesome portents of their imminent fate were splattered all around the church. It was the worst thing they had ever seen. The cowboys wanted to do something. They wanted to draw their pistols and murder all the bandits. But the silver statues were in their hands and more money than they had ever seen stuffed their saddlebags. A terrible choice tore their consciences. But they were just three.

The Jefe studied them closely, his feral, animal eyes sizing them up and taking their measure, seeing what they were made of.

Bodie looked at Fix.

Fix looked at Tucker.

Tucker eyed both of them. "There's too many of 'em. We can't help these people. Let's go."

Decision made.

Walking to their saddlebags on the floor with the empty clink of the spurs on their boots in the silent cathedral, they packed the statues of the Blessed Virgin in the treasure-filled pouches and lashed them tight.

CHAPTER EIGHT

PILAR WATCHED THE CHURCH.

It sat across the village up on the hill, too quiet.

The girl lay on her belly on the opposite ridge above the valley, peering from behind the rocks, occasionally glancing through the binoculars Tucker left her. All was still. She waited for gunshots, for screams, for some disturbance within the walls of any kind, but for nearly an hour there had been nothing. The last movement she had seen was the two bandits coming outside and taking the gunfighters' saddlebags from their tethered horses behind Santa Sangre, then going back inside. The big oaken doors had closed, and she had gotten a bad feeling. Her unease had begun as she had watched the cowboys ride up the hill, surrounded by so many bandits, and saw with her own eyes how outnumbered they were. Below the white adobe walls and steeple, it was so still there was not even a bird. Her town lay at the base of the hill, quiet as a grave. The girl caught herself fingering her crucifix and noticed that she had been praying beneath her breath, unaware she was doing so. Lifting the binoculars to her eyes again, she scanned the front of the church through the eyepiece, the walls looming big and flat and the oaken doors tightly closed in the circle view of the twin lenses.

There was nothing to see, nothing to hear, nothing for her to do but wait and pray.

Probably, she figured, they were loading up the silver. Perhaps no gunfire was a good sign. It would take them thirty minutes, she guessed, to take all the treasure from the church and get it loaded up on their horses. But would the werewolves, or the bandits they became during the day, just let them walk out of there with the loot? Perhaps they would, because the creatures knew it could kill them and wanted it gone. Just giving it to the cowboys was an easy solution. But the evil ones were cunning and might know the gunfighters meant to kill them with it. Then they would scourge the shootists where they stood with their knives and machetes and that might have happened already. Now she was thinking too much, and fresh doubts about the soundness of her plan filled her with dread. More likely, the gunslingers would have to shoot their way out, but that hadn't happened yet. Pilar was driving herself crazy imagining the different things that could be occurring inside.

Get your hands busy, she told herself.

Keeping her head down, the peasant girl slid out of view of the church and rose to her feet. She brushed dirt and pebbles off her baggy clothes, and trod down the path toward the blacksmith's shop nestled in the gully. Her time would be better spent preparing the fire and the kiln and the tools, so that if and when the time came and the three bad men returned with the silver, they could set to work directly in making the bullets.

She glanced up at the sun, hanging at two o'clock in the sky. Sunset and moonrise lay about five hours off, she gauged, and there was much to do. Fear stabbed her insides as she walked toward the shed. This was her village's last chance. It was the last full moon of the month and she had a terrible feeling that the werewolves would kill everyone tonight. So many things could go wrong. The gunfighters could already be dead inside the church. Even if they got out with the silver, their hands on all that treasure could easily tempt them from returning with it to the blacksmith's shop and they may just ride off, stealing the priceless valuables to become rich men and live like kings, breaking their promise to her.

That was the chance she took.

It was the only chance she'd had.

God would provide.

She entered the shed, glad of the cool shade. As she stood in the doorway, she gazed at the big cast iron pot, to be used for the melting of the silver, sitting empty. The anvil sat beside it. The sledgehammer. The dangling chains and andirons and molds hanging from the wooden buttresses. This was all they had, all the equipment that was at their disposal to wage war on The Men Who Walk Like Wolves. The food dishes of the gunfighters sat on the ground, and the girl experienced a twinge of loneliness seeing them. Be strong, Pilar told herself.

There was nothing to do but wait.

Restless and reflective, the girl somberly wandered over to a corner of the shed with her sleeping roll and the small tied quilt of personal belongings she had taken from her home before dawn, to have them with her for comfort. She had figured she'd need to stay up at the blacksmith's shop during the gunfighters' visit to the town and had wanted a few things with her. She untied the blanket and laid it open. There was her cross of Lord Jesus. Her wristlet of turquoise beads she had been given by her grandmother. A small miniature of her mother.

And there were the yellowed dime novels.

A large pile of them.

Her attention went there, to her treasures. With a growing smile, her eyes widened as they always had as she thumbed through the tattered pages, and her heart beat just a little faster.

DIME WESTERN MAGAZINE. COWBOY STORIES. ACE HIGH WESTERNS. FAR WEST MAGAZINE. The pulp novel covers were illustrated in vibrant colors, displaying lurid paintings of gunfighters and outlaws firing smoking guns spitting blazing muzzle fire and clutching buxom wenches behind them protectively. She had learned how to read English from these dime books when she was a child. The friendly Tennessee priest had brought them from the post office in town. He'd mail ordered the pulps because he'd seen how the small child's eyes lit up when he told her tales of the cowboys he'd met on his journeys. The minister's clever plan had worked, because from age five, little Pilar had devoured the penny dreadfuls with their romanticized melodramas of the big, powerful, heroic but gentle outlaws who were the heroes of the open range. It had formed her fantasy of the cowboy. Her overheated imagination was fueled by purple prose of desperate shootouts between evildoers and the tall, handsome, soft-spoken stranger who always had honor and never backed down from a fight. This was the thrilling bigger than life world she dreamed of beyond the impoverished confines of her humble village. The fantasy world western heroes were as much her companions as the simple farmers who were her friends and family. She wanted more than what her circumstances offered. Pilar yearned for the manly strength of the gunfighters she read of in the western pulps, dreamed of being swept away in the arms of such a man and kissed passionately, then bearing his child. But she knew she could not marry a man such as this or tie him down, for he was a restless rover and must always ride on into the sunset for more adventures. But he would always love her, and the child she bore would grow up to be a man of courage and bravery just like his father and become a hero like him. When Pilar became a teenager and the good reverend had given her adult classics to read, she would still keep the western books under her bed and reread them dozens of times until she had memorized each and every word. As she grew to a woman, she set aside childish things. But the cowboy remained in her heart.

When the werewolves came to her town, she knew at once the kind of strong, brave, fierce heroes she must find to protect her village, and realized it must have been God's plan to have her read dime novels as a child, memorizing them as she did the scripture. She would know at first sight the cowboy gunfighter who would deliver them.

That morning, standing across the street from Tucker, Pilar had known he was this man from the first moment she laid eyes upon him.

The girl tied the books back in the quilt. Kneeling, she gathered up some firewood and stuffed it under the heavy cast iron kettle. Briefly, she debated the wisdom of starting the fire now, knowing the chimney smoke might be seen by the bandits stationed around the church across the way, but she had not seen any of them outside, and the gunfighters would be back soon with the silver if they returned at all. Pilar lit the match. Rich scented smoke began to fill the structure as the flames began to lick. She looked around for what else needed to be prepared. The water cask was empty. Picking it up, she walked to the doorway.

Someone blocked her path.

The tall bandit was lean, wiry and feral. His face was long and stretched, vulpine in bone structure. His sharp teeth razored into a bad grin as he brushed a lock of oily, lank, filthy hair from his face. His predatory, wary eyes fixed her just the way the wolves she had seen did, always sizing you up. "*Buenas dias.*"

Pilar backed off as the one she had heard called Calderon by the Jefe pried the empty cask from her fingers and tossed it aside, advancing, corralling her back into the shed.

"*Hola*," the girl managed, thinking to avert her eyes submissively but not daring to let him out of her gaze. The bandit did not immediately make his intentions known, although he radiated a hungry animal smell and predatory heat. His thin lips drew back in a sneer over his big, chipped buck teeth as he eyeballed her.

The girl suddenly wanted to pee badly.

He was enjoying intimidating her, taking his time. The bandit ran a finger over one of the dishes the gunfighters had used, then ran his finger and its broken jagged nail on the anvil with the sledgehammer placed atop it, ready to be used.

The grating sound of the fingernail on steel hurt her ears and jangled her nerves.

Still Calderon watched her, mordant eyes black as pitch, impossible to read but observant and circumspect as they studied her.

When she could bear it no more, she said, "What do you want?"

His voice was high and nasally, and had a musical lilt. "These men, gunfighters, show up here. Just riding through they say. There is nothing here. Nothing anywhere near here. And yet they are here in this village. Chance, it could be, perhaps, but I think not. It is no accident they are here, *si*?" Pilar froze as the stalking Calderon slowly paced the blacksmith's shop, studying the metal forging equipment. He picked up a poker and tapped it on his hand. "This place. It is used to make metal. Harnesses. Plows for the fields. Or bullets, *si*?"

"Please, I don't understand." The girl cringed, knowing if she tried to flee the bandit would be on her in less than a second, tearing her asunder. She knew too well what they were capable of. He radiated violence and suspicion, but barely spoke above a whisper.

"What I think, *punta*, is men like these, they are here for the silver. Why else gringos come to a shit town like this? *Mucho dinero.*" He wagged his finger at her and made a scolding *tsk tsk* sound. "And I know you went and found them. Yes you did. Brought them here to kill us. Promised them *mucho* silver. Told them they needed the silver to kill *mis hermanos.*"

"I didn't."

And then he was there.

Across the room so fast she never saw him move.

His face was in hers, his dirty talon of a hand gripping her neck in a stranglehold and cutting off her respiration as she choked under the stink of him.

"Yes, *si?*"

"Yes." She could not lie.

"*Bueno.*"

And Pilar wept.

It was over.

Calderon would go back and tell his Jefe and the gunfighters would be ripped to shreds before they ever got out with the silver. She had tried. But had only been responsible for more deaths.

He reached out his hand and put it in her shirt, scooping out one of her bare breasts and squeezing it roughly in his fingers, thumbing her nipple painfully. Pilar didn't dare move, and terror spread through her that he would take the virginity she had protected so long.

Calderon watched her. "I am right, *si?*" He tugged her boob like a cow udder.

"*Si.*"

He released her breast. "I go now and tell Jefe. And we will kill them for you very nice. Then, tonight, I will be back, when the moon is up and you will open wide for me, *punta.*" With that, he extended his long foul tongue and lapped it like a dog across the side of her face.

She turned from him, wincing in disgust.

With a grunt of base satisfaction, Calderon stormed out of the blacksmith's shop, swung into his saddle and rode hard for the church.

Inside the defiled chapel, Tucker, Bodie and Fix had loaded their saddlebags to overflowing with the gleaming silver artifacts.

They were grabbing the last ornate candlesticks when Tucker noticed the scabrous, lean bandit with the wolfish face slink into the cathedral through the bright opening in the doors and skulk over to the Jefe. Giving the gunfighters the stink eye from across the pews, the lurking Calderon pressed his snout of a mouth to the bandit leader's ear and furtively whispered, a susurration canine in timbre. Mosca listened, nodded and watched the cowboys steadily without blinking. Sound carried in the cathedral but all Tucker could discern was the hissing whispering noises from Calderon. However, he heard Mosca's grinning response just fine. "*Comprendo, hermano.* I knew the minute they rode in." He wasn't sure that meant trouble or not, but Tucker figured they better make tracks. Ready to leave, the gunslingers were about to heave the saddlebags over their shoulders when they looked up and saw the Jefe standing, blocking the open doorway, silhouetted against the lowering sun. "Just one thing you must do for me before you go, amigos."

Tucker lowered the saddlebag and stood upright, facing Mosca. "What would that be?"

"Give me a gunfight."

"You and me?"

"*Si.* If you are faster than me, then you may go with the silver."

Bodie snorted. "Knew there was a catch."

"Here we go," muttered Fix.

"Fair enough." Tucker nodded to Mosca. Lowering his hands to his sides, fingers hovering by the stock of his pistol in his holster, Tucker assumed the position. He shot a glance for Bodie and Fix to back off as he stood in the center aisle between the pews and faced the Jefe standing with his arms crossed in front of the door. You could hear a pin drop. The other two gunfighters braced for the battle they were ready for when they first stepped into Santa Sangre. Each turned to face the army of bandits on either side of the church who were slowly stepping near their rifles and pistols, watching them like a pack of hungry wolves, beady eyes on the gunfighters' hands perched by their holstered irons.

None of the banditos went for their weapons. The gunslingers were closer to their pistols and would get the initial shots off and draw first blood before the place turned into a shooting gallery.

Mosca spoke softly, facing off for the showdown with Tucker, yet his arms remained calmly crossed. "Your move."

As they faced off for the shoot-out, Tucker put the army of bandits surrounding him out of his mind because his friends had them covered. He focused on sizing up his adversary and took his measure. In his sightline, he saw nothing in his own straight-ahead stare but the bandit leader and his guns, taking in every movement of his opponent. The hirsute man was fat and ungainly, yet his locked gaze was supremely confident and assured, primal and raw as a wild coyote. He seemed to be enjoying the prospect of imminent death, and that was just a little damn unnerving. It was the crazy ones you worried about. Tucker waited to draw, he could wait a long time.

Hell with it. Nobody lives forever.

It happened in a split second.

Tucker drew first, fist closing on the gunstock, feeling the tug of the barrel leaving its sheath. Instantly, the muzzle was pointed forward, his right hand pushing the gun and hammer under the flattened palm of his left hand, fanning and firing a shot right between Mosca's eyes. The bullet put a neat red hole in the Jefe's forehead, spritzing a spray of matter behind his head. The bandit leader remained standing with his arms crossed. The gunshot echoed in sonic reverberation through the church, scattering a few vultures. No further shots rang forth.

Tucker expected the air to explode with gunfire. He looked left and right with his pistol drawn but the bandits were just standing there on all sides, grinning. The air was taut with tension as Bodie and Fix stood braced, ready to draw on all the other brigands but none of them made a move. He threw glances to his comrades but they were staring in the direction of the Jefe with their mouths hanging open.

Mosca just stood there, shot in the head.

Tucker watched him, the barrel of his raised pistol drifting smoke. There was a tidy, penny-sized hole in the forehead of the man.

Mosca's eyes popped open, daylight glinting off the rows of gold teeth as his lips spread in an insane grin.

"You got me, amigo." With that, the Jefe drew his pistol.

Tucker quickly shot him five times, fanning and firing his pistol until it clicked empty, the bullets slamming home into Mosca's chest in a tight pattern that tore cloth and spurted blood.

"Oh! Ow! Ow! Oh!" the bullet-ridden bandit cried in mock pain. He stayed on his feet, dancing a little jig. The Jefe was laughing the whole time, unharmed. "I let you win again, amigo. *Mira*. As you can see, bullets do not hurt us. We live forever. We are the strong. You can be like us. Impossible to kill. Men like you should ride with us. Join us."

Tucker, Bodie and Fix exchanged slow glances.

"*Join us*." Those words hung in the air.

Tucker heard the sound of flies growing louder and louder. The cloying noise of the insects seemed to emanate from the leader of the brigands, as if the hive was inside his guts. And right then the cowboy understood these were not men. Bullets could not kill them. Nothing could.

The gunfighters were struck dumb, faced with *hombres* whom bullets did not faze.

Fix showed rare wide-eyed shock. "It was true what that damn peasant said about these sumbitches."

"Every damn word of it," Bodie stammered.

Before their eyes, the bullet hole in Mosca's head healed, the penetrated flesh closing up as the cauterized blood ceased to drip, leaving barely a scar. "So what do you say?"

Tucker realized what the Jefe offered the gunfighters was to make them invulnerable, immortal, impervious to death by gun or noose, as the bandits obviously were. An end to fear and worry. At once, he felt utterly trail weary as Mosca's eyes fixed on his own, looking through his head across the desecrated church in a persuasive comfort of fellowship. Why not join the bandits, the cowboy wondered, what did they have to lose? Nothing but their humanity, but how much of that burdensome commodity did they have left anyway? They'd killed, robbed, cheated, left numbers too great to count dying in the dirt and that was all that lay ahead in their future until a bullet did them in. He and his two companions were little more than animals now anyway, ready to take the treasure and abandon the villagers to slaughter even though they had given their word, all three of them, that they would protect the people. It was so easy to just go for the money. Life for him was nothing but the same base, dirty, dismal day-to-day survival it was for any lizard that ever crawled out from under a rock. He took in the feral, hairy faces that minutes earlier had seemed so foul and now looked strong, admirable and reassuringly kindred and familiar. His brothers. Their terrible stench was the same, but it no longer bothered him any more than his own bad smell. Hell, if they joined up with this lot they wouldn't even have to shave anymore, or bathe. His gaze traveled to the naked girls huddled in the corner and saw their welted asses and bruised breasts and the iron in his trousers rose, because he wanted their bodies and suddenly he didn't mind the blood.

The two gunfighters on either side shrugged amiably when he glanced at them, like they could go either way, but they were looking to Tucker to make the decisions like they usually did.

What did they have to live for anyway? The last few years the three outlaws had been relentlessly hunted, on the run, fearing death by hanging or bullets, suffering starvation, scrounging for a buck. What good was the silver? Tucker wondered. Even if they got out of here with the treasure, people would be gunning for them trying to take it. He might even have to keep his eyes on Bodie and Fix in case they got greedy, and sleep with one eye open at night in case one of them tried to plug him and take it all. They could never go north back to America again, not with the reward on their heads and The Cowboys would never relent. They had no home, no family, no friends except each other until now. Until these bandits. Their home was here. Mosca's gaze had a spellbinding effect. Not like he was a friend, more that he was inevitable, cut from the same stock as they were, and his will had a powerful pull. Tucker beheld Bodie and Fix clenching their guns at half-mast, flickers of indecision in his comrades' eyes and he knew, without asking, that they felt it too. The three gunslingers stood side by side in the aisle between the pews, the looming shadows of the bandits on all sides in the shadowy recesses of a church no longer a place of worship for a Christian God but a terrible pagan and nameless deity. Tucker had often worried whether they were good or bad men, but now knew there was no good or bad, just what you were capable of. These bandits were capable of anything. Like the Jefe said, they were the strong, and the respect in his gaze showed them his pack was where they belonged. Take the bandit's offer. No more fear. Be free. Pure. Indulge their appetites like animals and eat when hungry, fuck when lustful, kill when bloodthirsty. The blood was the thing. Best of all, not to care anymore. Nothing left to care about. Let it all go. Being a man was a pain in the damn ass. It was all about survival. And these bastards had survived forever, Tucker knew, and so could they.

The pathetic muffled sobbing from the back of the church drifted through the recesses of the cathedral, sounding over the blood pounding in Tucker's ears that had been all he had been hearing. It was a sound of raw terror. It stirred his conscience, made him cognizant of the poor people, mothers, fathers, children, waiting to be butchered like livestock. Somewhere deep inside him, some stubborn long-buried grain of humanity asserted itself. The cowboy knew this pain and struggle was his, and Tucker did not want to lose himself.

He broke Mosca's gaze, ending the spell. The silver gleamed in his eyes, and greed and fortune became all consuming. He had more money in his hands than he had ever known, and their job here was almost done, if they could just get out in one piece.

"Thanks, amigo, maybe next time," he said to the bandit leader.

Mosca just watched him.

Then he shrugged with a tinge of atavistic melancholy and regret in his gravelly voice. "Suit yourself."

Tucker kept his voice even. "Just take 'er real easy, pardners." He looked at his companions. "Grab the silver. We're gettin' out of here."

Mosca stood aside to give them wide berth, displaying to them his gold grin the whole time. As the gunfighters walked out the front doors of Santa Sangre with their saddlebags laden with untold riches, the bandit leader said four final words in parting. "You will be back."

And the three gunfighters fled the church of The Men Who Walk Like Wolves without looking back, shaken to their spurs as they tied their saddlebags to their horses, swinging into their stirrups and riding out of the hellish place. Their three horses left trails of dust in their wake as they galloped down the hill through the town away from Santa Sangre, hard charging up the ravine and hurtling out into the desert wastes of Durango. Even over their thundering hooves they could hear the ringing laughter of the bandits on the wind after they were miles away.

Tucker didn't feel better until he and his gang had covered ten miles and even then he didn't look back.

❨

Mosca stood in the doorway of the church, his black eyes glinting, chewing a toothpick, considering the three receding dust trails of the gunfighters in the distance.

The vulpine Calderon walked up to him, watching the cowboys go, displeased.

Mosca's eyes and voice were blank. "They will come back."

Calderon shook his head grimly. "I think not, Jefe."

Mosca's eyes looked up, boiling with blood. "They will because you will bring them back, slung over their saddles."

The second in command bandito turned to his leader and his chapped lips pulled wide over cracked, jagged teeth. "I have been waiting for your word, Jefe."

"I know, *pendejo*, I know."

"Which pieces of them do you wish for me to bring you?"

"The meaty parts. And get our fucking silver!"

With a leathery chuckle, the hulking and hairy Calderon tugged himself into his saddle with one fist. He grabbed and loaded four bolt action Henry rifles in his saddle bags, stuffing in several more ammo belts. Mosca tossed him two Colt Dragoon pistols which the bandit crammed in his belt, beside the two guns in his sideholsters. The bandit was armed to the teeth, and in a killing mood. "*Gracias, Jefe. Me gusta muerto los hombres.*"

"They are all yours, amigo."

With a wild whoop, Calderon stabbed his spurred heels into his horse's flanks and charged down the hill, off into the distance in pursuit of the fading trails of dust of his prey.

CHAPTER NINE

"*YOU WILL BE BACK.*"

Tucker banished Mosca's farewell words from his mind, urging his horse faster. The gunfighter never again wanted to set eyes on that unholy church and what lay within. Like Lot's wife, the cowboy feared if he looked back, saw but a tiny glimpse of the distant steeple, he would turn to naught. The three gunfighters galloped across the hot griddle of the desert, the baking wind smashing against them, and they leaned into their horses and heard the galloping hooves and the *rattleclank* of their treasure-laden leather saddlebags, making fast their souls and good their escape. Open badland wastes beckoned and embraced, and soon they were far from that accursed village.

Tucker thought of the silver. He thought of how he would spend it. But try as he might, the cowboy couldn't get out of his mind the little figure of the peasant girl standing on the ridge as they charged past on their horses with their stolen silver, watching them go. Even at the great distance, just from the brief glance he gave her, he saw the slump of her shoulders.

He had been many things in his time. Son. Cowboy. Husband. Widower. Soldier. Outlaw. Thief. Killer.

Now liar.

Samuel Llewellyn Tucker wondered when it was exactly he had gotten too mean to pray.

It had been an hour since she saw those sons of bitches ride out with the silver and all hope was lost.

This is why when Pilar heard the horse's hooves below the ridge heading into town, her heart leapt in her bosom. Had the gunfighters had a change of heart and returned to fulfill their promise? Her stomach quickly fell as she rushed to the edge of the incline and peered down to see only a lone rider on a horse trotting into the village. It wasn't them. It was as she feared; they had abandoned her and stolen the silver that would have saved her people. But as she squinted through the shimmery dust, she recognized the rider.

It was Vargas, the old town drunk who had fled the village on a whisky binge years before.

What was he doing back?

The *borracho* rode into town armed to the teeth with silver bullets.

He was betting that The Men Who Walked Like Wolves didn't know that.

His old tired bones ached in his saddle from the long ride, but his heart was strong. The sight of his abandoned, derelict village shocked and dismayed him. It was a graveyard for vultures and flies. As he led his horse through the deserted corrals and stalls and saw the bones and rotting meat he knew they belonged to his friends. How many still survived he did not know.

But some must have.

For the bandits still occupied the area.

Up on the hill, by the church they now blasphemously called Santa Sangre, he could already see a few distant stick figures of the cutthroats patrolling the perimeter of the stark white mission. The whole place stank of death. His horse feared the area and sensed the unnatural evil present. It tossed its head in its bridle and wanted to go no further, but the old man held firmly on the bit with an iron grip and urged the *caballo* forward. Just a few more yards, then he would dismount and cut it loose, and his own feet would carry him the rest of the way.

He had a lifetime of dishonor to make up for.

The village, or what was left of it, was depending on him.

He would not let them down.

Perhaps the old man should have considered his age, his eyesight. Perhaps he should have been mindful of the bandits' sheer numbers compared to the amount of bullets he had. But this was not on his mind.

At the edge of town, the *borracho* dismounted and unstrapped his saddlebags and firearms that were already loaded with the bullets that would kill the werewolves. He thanked his horse for the good service it provided and before he could smack it on the rump, the stallion took off out of the village at a heated gallop, wanting to be gone from the evil place. The old man stuffed the Navy and SAA pistols in his belt, slung a Mexican bolt action rifle over his right shoulder and a Winchester repeater rifle over his left. He stuffed handfuls of silver bullets he had already separated by caliber into different pockets. They were heavy and the guns and ammo weighed him down, but he bore up under the greater burden of responsibility.

Walking to the base of the hill, the *borracho* faced the church like a gunfighter. A rifle he held on one hand, a pistol in the other. The old timer stuck out his chest. Raised his chin. He was not afraid. It was a good day to die.

"WEREWOLVES, SHOW YOURSELVES SO I MAY SEND YOU TO HELL!" he shouted boldly.

The bandits looked down, taken aback at the sight of the decrepit stranger down the hill. Vargas bellowed at them as they noticed him for the first time. "TODAY YOU DIE! ALL OF YOU! I, HECTOR VARGAS, HAVE COME TO KILL YOU AND FREE MY PEOPLE!"

The fat, bearded leader of the brigands stepped out of the open wooden doors. He blinked in the sunshine but also in incredulity at the one old man in the village outskirts below yelling up at him in challenge. Mosca cracked a big gold-toothed grin. The four bandits flanking him by the church also grinned. They laughed mockingly, arms crossed, for this was very funny to them.

The *borracho* blushed in humiliation and his legs shook at the ridicule, but he stood his ground, unshouldering his rifle. "I AM HERE TO RELEASE MY PEOPLE! I AM HERE TO KILL YOU COWARDS!" His frail voice barely reached the animals on the hill above, but they heard enough to laugh even harder, busting a gut.

Shaking his head, the amused bandit leader cupped his hands over his mouth. "Who are you, old fool?" he shouted.

"I AM HECTOR VARGAS AND I WAS BORN IN THIS VILLAGE! AS MY FATHER WAS BORN HERE AND HIS FATHER BEFORE HIM! THIS IS MY HOME!"

"But why have you come back?" Mosca's voice sounded astonished at the audacity of the old timer.

"THIS IS MY HOME AND THESE ARE MY PEOPLE WHOSE BLOOD YOU HAVE SPILT AND I HAVE COME TO KILL YOU AND SEND EACH AND EVERY ONE OF YOU STRAIGHT TO HELL! YOU HEAR ME, WEREWOLVES? I, HECTOR VARGAS, HAVE COME TO KILL YOU!"

Mosca spread his arms generously, displaying his chest. "Get on with it then!" he chortled.

Fired up with purpose, the old man shouldered the repeater, took aim and fired right at the chest of the bandit leader. His arms were frail, his eyesight poor and his aim was a little off. The bullet struck Mosca in the right shoulder instead and made a blossoming red bloom. But while the bullet missed the heart by a foot, it wiped the grin right off the bandit's face and the sudden raw fear and agony the *borracho* saw in the brigand's eyes emboldened him.

"SILVER!" screamed Mosca in utter surprise and unbearable anguish as he pawed the big wound in his shoulder, the impacted slug burning like a red-hot poker buried in his flesh. He fell back against the wall, howling in pain like a wild animal. Tugging his knife from his belt, he jabbed it into the ragged hole, trying to dig the slug out. "AAAGGG-GGGGGGGGGGHHHH!" The bandit leader fell to his knees, buckled over in panic, desperately prying the round out of his flesh with the knife. "HE HAS SILVER BULLETS!"

For one brief moment of glory, the old man had them. He opened fire on the other bandits, cocking his Winchester with one hand and firing his Colt in his other fist, unleashing a fusillade of silver bullets on the top of the hill. Spat out cartridge casings glinted gloriously in the sunlight as they flew twirling from the breech of his repeater. He rotated the rifle, cocking the lever action around his fingers, and fired from the hip, again and again. The slugs exploded and caromed off the white adobe walls of the church as the alarmed bandits ducked for cover. They scrambled for their weapons under the onslaught. One of them was hit in the kneecap and went down screaming in pathetic agony, a yelping sound more canine than human, pressing his own fingers into the bullet hole to pinch out the molten-hot silver slug.

It was the best moment of the old man's long life.

The three other bandits had snapped to attention and unholstered their pistols and rifles and began shooting back. Their aim was good for wolves have sharp vision.

The first round in the old man's side broke three of his ribs. He watched a foot-long jet of blood fountain from his shirt.

Still he laid down fire.

Bullets buzzed past his ears like a swarms of angry bees. The *borracho*'s SAA pistol was empty so he tossed it aside and drew his Navy revolver and kept firing. His arms ached from the recoil but his adrenaline was pumping. Slugs exploded geysers of dirt at his feet. He could see the muzzle flashes of the bandits shooting down on him from the hill through the chalky haze of plaster dust his own bullets had kicked up when they ricocheted off the walls of the church.

Mosca damn near sawed his shoulder off but he got the bullet out.

The red flattened slug clattered on the ground.

He kicked it in blind rage, roaring in fury, the pain in his shoulder subsiding now the silver was gone.

Instantly, the bandit leader was up on his feet, smoothly quick-drawing one of the revolvers from his cross holsters and squeezing off a single shot that blew the *borracho* clean off the ground. The bandit leader spat in the dust in vile contempt, raised his hand and his men stopped shooting. The ringing reverbs of the gunfire faded to silence as the brigands on the hill stared down at the sprawled figure of the old man down in the village below them.

He was moving.

The *borracho* lay on his back in the settling dust, his life bleeding out of him. He'd lost his guns. The weapons had flown from his grip when the shot that felled him blew a rat hole out of his thigh. He had taken two rounds, the other in his side. The old man coughed blood and grit his teeth, turning his head to see the pistol ten yards from him. There was still feeling in his arms and legs and he wasn't dead yet.

Get the gun.

With a grunt of pain, he rolled over onto his stomach and began to crawl for his weapon.

Quick, get the gun.

Mosca's eyes were vacant as he started walking down the hill, in no hurry. The smoking Colt was in his fist, carried loosely at his side. Step by step, he descended the gravel incline toward the pathetic figure on the ground below who crawled on his belly like a snail toward one of his guns with the silver bullets. The bandit leader took his time in his approach, face slack, grimy hair falling down his back. Mosca stuck a cigar in his mouth and fired it up with a stick match he struck with the thumb on his free hand. He blew clouds of smoke like a chimney, stogie clamped in his teeth as he spoke.

"You have heart, *pendejo*," he snarled. "I'll give you that." The wounded old shootist kept dragging himself toward the pistol in the dirt. The bandit leader descended from the church, smoking as he spoke. "I saw a mouse that had heart once. There was this big cat and she had pounced on this mouse, tore off his leg. The back leg. The mouse tried to crawl away, bleeding, without a leg." The bandit leader's boots had reached the base of the hill in a crumble of gravel. Mosca slowly and deliberately closed the distance between himself and the crawling man, talking softly. "The cat, she just watched him crawl and crawl without the leg and when the mouse was at the end of the porch thinking it would get away, the cat pounced again and dragged him back, biting off his other leg."

The *borracho* pulled and tugged and dragged himself across the punishing rocks and stones of the hard pack ground. His leg and sides were wet and sang with agony, and he left a smear of blood in his wake. The pistol was now three feet away. He saw his hand reach for it, fingers stretching the last few inches for the stock. Counted rounds in his head. Five more silver bullets were chambered. Then the large ugly shadow fell across him and the old man could smell the bandit leader standing right behind him.

The first shot split his eardrums.

The old man's right hand reaching for the gun disappeared in a fine red mist and shrapnel of bone fragments. The blasted stump of a wrist geysered a jet of blood a foot in the air. His own screaming drowned out the sound of the second gunshot that ricocheted in a flash of sparks off the pistol, sending the gun skittling another five yards away where it spun in a glint of metal in sunlight until it went still.

Mosca stood tall and awful over the old man who lay writhing in agony, clutching with his good hand his arm shot off at the wrist. The *borracho* spat up at him but the bloody saliva didn't reach its target and splattered back onto the old man's face. The bandit leader chuckled, enjoying this, puffing cigar smoke. Gritting his teeth, steeling his gaze, the wounded wretch twisted his head to regard the pistol a few yards farther from him now.

And began to crawl for it.

Reaching toward the fallen weapon with his last good hand.

"You have heart, *pendejo*. Like the mouse." Mosca smiled, nodding his approval. "How I remember the cat on the porch watching as the mouse, now without two legs, pulled himself across the porch with both its front legs, inch by inch, leaving a long trail of little mouse blood. It went *squeak squeak*. The cat, she just waited, for she had nothing better to do." The bandit blew wafting smoke from the muzzle of his *pistola*, and took another step to keep pace with the maimed man desperately dragging himself on his stomach toward the gun. The old man's revolver was now two feet from his left-hand fingers.

"*Squeak squeak*, eh little mouse?"

Still the old man crawled, dragged, urged himself toward his pistol with his last remaining strength, suffering terribly. Towering above, taking his sweet time, his murderer coldly regarded the side of the *borracho*'s face, watching the drunk bite his lip bloody to stop himself from passing out. Another foot now. The slow drag of shirt on gravel. Those aged fingers stretching for the barrel of the gun with all the force of will their owner could muster to fire just one more silver bullet if he could. Fingertips six inches away. "Can you guess what happened next, *pendejo*, do you even care? I know you must focus now on getting that gun, so I will tell you. The mouse with the big heart, he made it again to the edge of the porch and another inch he would be safe when the cat pounced, dragged him back and bit off his front leg." Relishing the moment, squeezing every last drop of sadistic pleasure out of it, Mosca slid his revolver back in his holster.

The drunk's ancient tobacco-yellowed fingertips touched steel.

The bandit spun his pistol out of his holster around his forefinger and fired a single quick shot from the hip, blowing the *borracho*'s left hand clean off. Finger pieces and bits of palm flesh splattered the dirt as the old man wailed dismally, holding up a gruesome soup of a hand-less wrist out of which jagged a splintered bone.

"My problem, and your problem, is that I am not a cat, I am a wolf."

Mosca moved with lightning speed and with one filthy fist grabbed the old man by his thinning white hair, brutally yanking his head up and lifting his shoulders off the ground with savage force.

"And a wolf goes for the throat."

With that, Mosca sheathed his gun and drew out his knife, sawing at the *borracho*'s neck. The blade cut deep into the flesh, gushing blood in all directions. The bandit's feral visage was splattered with the bright red oxygenated arterial spray and his grinning teeth turned crimson in a face that was a lurid mask of gore. The dying man's eyes bulged in unimaginable horror as in his remaining seconds of consciousness he felt his own head being cut off. Mosca viciously jerked the blade back and forth, slicing through skin, tendon, muscle and finally spinal cord with a sickening *crack* and the torso began to fall away, held to the head by a long, wet rope of meat. Grunting impatiently, the bandit leader shook the nearly severed head violently in his grip, until the last grisly strand of muscle snapped and the skull came loose. He carried it by the hair over to a corral fence and slammed the ragged neck stump down on a jutting wooden post, grotesquely impaling the decapitated head. Its sightless eyes stared glassily. Mosca wiped the blade clean on the dead man's hair then sheathed it, his own gaze as detached as the head. "*Si*, you had heart, *pendejo*. Too bad for you it's over there."

The bandit leader kicked the headless trunk out of his way as he trod back up the hill to Santa Sangre.

"Fuck you and your silver."

Up above on the ridge, tears poured down Pilar's cheeks watching the scene below from her hiding place. She had seen the whole savage and brutally sadistic killing. Made herself watch. Yet had done nothing. What good could she have done? she told herself over and over. Had she showed herself, with certainty she would have been captured and raped and killed and eaten like the rest. But while her reasoning was sound, the peasant girl knew in her heart she was a coward and she was afraid and that old man who had died so badly down there had not been afraid to die, to do what he could. *You are no hero, Pilar. You have learned there are no heroes, just the strong who prey on the weak.* Shame and self-disgust consumed Pilar and she felt small and worthless as she slunk back from the ridge into the hard lengthening shadows of the lowering sun.

The old man down there at least had been brave.

It made his flesh that much tastier to the vultures who even now descended to feed on his remains.

Then it hit her. The dead man had been using silver bullets, and somewhere on his corpse he likely had more rounds. The body was out in the open in the square. As soon as the bandits went back inside the church she decided she would sneak down into the town and retrieve the silver rounds and the weapons to fire them, staying out of sight. It was up to Pilar now to rescue her sister and her mother, though she would certainly die in the attempt. Her promise had been to return for Bonita, not live forever. She could be brave still.

A few minutes later, the girl risked a peek over the edge of the ridge and saw the two bandits collecting all the unused silver bullets and guns from the dead old man, scavenging the body of weapons like the vultures were of its flesh. The carrion birds did not even pause in their feeding as the brigands took the last of the ammo that could kill them back up into Santa Sangre and all hope was once again lost.

That's when she saw her little sister step out of the church hand in hand with the bandit leader and for the first and only time in her life, Pilar prayed for her own death.

"Sit with me."

"Okay."

The big man with the bad smell sat on the edge of the hill, eye level with the child. "Sit on my lap." Bonita watched him a moment. He was smiling, patting his thigh. So she sat on him. He put his dirty paw of a hand gently on her back as she perched on his knee. They looked out at the quiet village, and for a while neither spoke.

He did first. "It is cool up here, *si*?"

"The breeze is nice." She nodded.

"It blows your hair like a dandelion." Mosca sniffed her hair in a way that was odd to her. "You have beautiful hair, child."

"Thank you."

He stroked her black tresses. She wrinkled her nose. "You smell bad."

Mosca chuckled. "But you smell very, very good. So good I will eat you." He laughed and she did too, like it was a game. "You are a good girl, *si*?"

She shrugged. He held her on his lap under the hot sun of the day. "You are a bad man," she stated firmly. "And you have dirty fingernails."

The bandit roared with laughter. "I like you, child. You are very brave to speak to me in such a manner. What is your name?"

"Bonita."

"Such a pretty name."

The little girl thanked him politely, perfectly behaved.

"Are you not scared of me?"

She shook her head. "No."

His reddened eyes twinkled with mirth. "Why is this, my brave little one?"

"Because my sister will come and save me."

He lifted an eyebrow. "Will she? And where is your sister now?"

"I don't know."

"But I do." With a wolfish grin, he nudged his bearded jaw toward the ridge across the village. "She is right over there, at the blacksmith's shop. Do you know what she is doing at this very minute as we speak?"

"Getting ready to come and save me."

"Watching us right now. We can't see her because she hides, but she sees you. Wave to her." The bandit lifted the little girl's hand and they both waved. "That's it. Wave hello." The child waved for a while, then put her arm down.

"Do you think she saw me?" Bonita asked.

"Certainly. She is crying right now, because she knows that all is lost. Your big sister is very brave, like you. She rode very far to bring dangerous *vaqueros* to kill us, but she chose poorly and those men stole the silver. They were very bad men."

"Worse than you?"

"Much worse because they lied. I am bad, but I do not lie."

"I'm sad now."

The bandit stared in her face with gentleness. "I had a beautiful little girl just like you once. You remind me of her."

"Did she die?"

He nodded somberly. "She was about your age."

"What was her name?"

"I don't remember."

The little girl looked at him perplexed, like he was kidding her. "How can you forget your child's name?"

His eyes were distant now. "Because it was a long, long time ago."

She fidgeted. He adjusted her position on the loose pants on his muscled thigh to make her more comfortable. "How long?"

He regarded her with melancholy. "Five hundred years."

"People don't live to be five hundred years old."

"No, people don't."

"So how can your child have been five hundred years ago?"

"Because I am not People. I think you know this."

"Yes."

He touched her face.

Sniffed her skin.

Tears began to flow from her eyes.

"Don't be sad, little one. Everybody dies. This is as it should be."

He stood.

"One day you will, too," he said. The bandit held out his hand. "I will take you back to your mother."

Bonita rose and took his hand and together they walked back into the church. "My sister is coming."

"Perhaps."

"My sister, when she comes, she will kill you."

The little girl looked up at the huge bandit with her honest button eyes.

He didn't blink.

All he said was . . .

"I know."

The bloody bullet wound of a sun sunk into a lake of gore on the horizon as gathering darkness extinguished the last traces of any hope of day. The desert at dusk stretched endlessly on all sides, claustrophobic in its sheer vastness. Three distant riders rested their horses and trotted toward a box canyon of crevices and towering rock crags.

Far to the rear, hanging back, a fourth horse and rider pursued them with the dogged dour determination of a coyote. Like the ageless desert predator he was, the hunter blended into the landscape and stayed out of sight.

The gunfighters had been on the trail for three hours, retracing their steps from the long morning ride from the cantina because without a map of the area they didn't know where they were, and a wrong turn in the endless desert with its lethal heat was a death warrant. Plus, their own sign was still fresh and easy to follow. They'd decided to head west once they reached the stagecoach trail they'd encountered earlier, and from there follow it south. The Wells Fargo line would be routed to civilization. The men took it easy on their horses because the animals were weighed down with the brimming saddlebags of silver. If they lost any of the mounts, they'd have to rig up a drag for some of the treasure and that would slow them considerably. It had been about 3:00 p.m. when the men had ridden out of Santa Sangre, and night was fast approaching, so they began looking for a place to camp and start out fresh first thing the next morning. That box canyon ahead looked as good a place as any. Tucker said again what he had said every half an hour since they fled. "Too damn easy."

Fix was in an expansive mood. "We're rich, boys. What you gonna do with your'n?"

Bodie sucked some whisky from his bottle. "Buy me some pussy," he belched.

"Then after that what?"

"I dunno. Buy me s'more."

The silver clinked and clanked like a tambourine in time with their spurs and saddle cleats.

"You're gonna spend it all on pussy, Bodie?"

"No, I ain't gonna spend it all on pussy neither, Fix. I'm gonna buy other stuff. Like clothes. And a new gun probably. Then I'm gonna . . . well I'm gonna . . . put it in a bank, that's what I'm gonna do, so's I can have my money working for me while I figure out what to spend it on *besides pussy*!"

He cracked up hysterically, and Fix joined in the laughter.

The little, taut gunslinger's eyes went distant. "Figure mebbe I'll buy me a little spread down Durango way. Get me some cattle. Settle down . . . mebbe."

Tucker shook his head, holding his reins, hips shifting with the horse's gait on the saddle. "Lot of money, boys, that silver is a whole lot of money." He was preoccupied, riding in the lead ahead, eyes hard in the distance. "And all it's given us so far is a big set of brand new problems."

"Like what?" asked Bodie. "We're rich."

"That's if'n we live to spend it. We got to be real careful. Right now we're riding through no man's land with a fortune. We can't just ride around Mexico carrying all this silver. What we need to do is bury it. I say we split the loot into three parcels and we each ride out and hide it where the others don't know about."

Tucker felt the unfamiliar twinge of distrust in the air between the three men.

"Reckon this much *dinero* could be a big temptation even twixt the best of friends," Fix grimly agreed.

"It ain't that exactly," Tucker said, although now the specter of betrayal had been raised it lay in the air like a dead fart, ruining the mood. "What I mean is we split up and each bury a third of the silver. Let's say one of us gets caught somehow with his parcel of silver and the sumbitches try to beat out of him the location of the rest of the treasure, he can't spill what he don't know."

"Can't argue with that." Fix grunted in agreement.

Bodie nodded, eyes glazed in confusion from trying to follow the conversation.

Tucker continued. "Then after we bury it, we regroup. Each of us knows where his parcel of the treasure is and doesn't tell the others. And the agreement is that each of the buried shares is owned three ways by us, so if we lose one, nobody's out of pocket. Agreed?" They others nodded. "It's decided then. We bury the treasure and we bury it soon. Tomorrow. That's one problem licked."

"So we just ride back and dig up what we need?" Bodie asked.

"That's the idea. Problem two. We can't go around cashing silver candlesticks and religious articles. They'll make us for thieves, and we got enough people after us already. What we need to do is melt this silver down into bars. So we got to locate a blacksmith's shop directly like that town back there had. We'll pay the blacksmith a share for his work and his silence. If we think he's dodgy, we'll just kill him when he's done the work."

"A bullet's a lot cheaper than a share of the silver, I savvy." Fix clicked his teeth. Tucker knew right then that the as yet unidentified blacksmith already had a slug of lead with his name on it.

"Mebbe so. We go back one at a time, dig up one parcel of silver goods from the church at a time, bring it back have the blacksmith melt it. The other two can remain with him to be sure he don't run off with our loot. Once we get these artifacts melted down into bricks, then each of us ride out and bury their share same place or t'other."

"Then what?" Fix asked, because Tucker had a habit of thinking things through which was why he was unspoken leader of the tight-knit gang.

"Then we got the same problem. Can't go riding around with this much silver. Not unless we want to get robbed or killed. It's got to be a million dollars or more we're haulin' right now in our saddlebags. And unless we want to spend our remaining days in Durango, we can't leave it buried and just keep coming back for it piecemeal. I say we bank it in Juarez or Mexico City. Turn it, or some of it, over into cash in bank accounts. It'll take us a few weeks, with all the riding to the buried silver and the banks and back, but we take it real slow and careful and patient and we'll get 'er done."

"We got another problem," Fix offered. "All them federals and bounty hunters on our ass, and remember those banks likely have our posters up. Heading into a bank is a big damn risk."

"Mebbe we could pay off the Federales. Pay 'em the reward on us and a bonus for staying off our backs. Buy their protection," said Bodie. "Not like we ain't got the money. We can buy anything. Including our own asses."

Tucker and Fix looked at the third of their number. Once in a while, he made sense and when the normally dull man had one of his good ideas it was always a pleasant surprise. They nodded.

"That could work, we get to the right Federales," Tucker admitted. "Maybe that fat pig general Lopez who heads up the fort outside of Mexico City we had that run in with back in May. Bet a few bars of silver would persuade him to send the word have his troops back off. That would sure as shit piss off The Cowboys, but if the price was right, he'd probably string up any of their bounty hunters they send after us too."

"Then we just lay low in Mexico the rest of our days." Fix shrugged. "In the style to which I intend to become accustomed."

"Might be a good idea buy a big ass ranch or hacienda down Guadalajara way. Men is going to be coming for us, but we hire on some Mexican guards, pay off the Federales like Bodie said, we could buy protection and live behind the walls a lifetime. Or until they forget about us." They men of action considered the unpleasant prospect of being so penned up for eternity. It didn't sit.

"Right."

"Right."

"Whatever."

"Sure as shit can't go back to the U.S.," Fix agreed.

"Not any state got an extradition treaty with Arizona, we can't," Tucker said. "I hear Doc Holliday is still rotting away in a Leadville jail up in Colorado fighting extradition by the Tombstone boys and word is they're sending his ass back to The Cowboys and a waiting noose directly."

"Why the hell isn't Wyatt Earp helping his friend out?" Bodie wondered.

"Heard Earp dropped him like a hot potato after the Vigilante Raid," Tucker said ruefully.

"Earp was always a prick." Fix chuckled dismissively. "Should have put a bullet in his brain pan when I had the chance. Holliday too."

"We get our money banked, we might can risk New York, maybe San Francisco, set ourselves up as proper gentlemen or robber barons. Or we can catch a ship and head to England. Start over."

"Too much to think about right now." Fix rubbed his eyes. "Been a long day. Right now, I just want to set camp and break open a bottle of whisky and admire our spoils. Tomorrow, we'll bury it, just like you said, friend, and go find us that blacksmith."

Suddenly being rich wasn't sounding so great, Tucker was thinking. It was confusing and tense trying to figure out a way to hold onto their money and keeping what they stole looked harder than getting it in the first place. Nothing had changed. They were still going to feel hunted, still spend their lives looking over their shoulders, now more than ever.

And that wasn't all that was weighing heavy on his conscience.

"Hey, Tuck. What you gonna spend your share of all this loot on?" Bodie asked affably.

"Peace of mind."

"Huh?"

"Them poor wretches back there. We gave them a royal screwin', leaving 'em to those bastards."

Fix sneered. "Fuck 'em, Tucker. Them Mexicans was stupid enough to roll over for them bandits, stupid enough to tell us where their silver was, and a fool and his money are easily parted."

Tucker chuckled mirthlessly. "We parted 'em with it that's for sure."

The little wiry gunfighter was bothered. "You going soft all of a sudden?"

Tucker didn't take the bait. There was sadness and regret in his blue eyes. "Just wondering when exactly we became the bad guys is all."

Bodie shrugged. "We ain't no worst than most. I love my mama."

"My mama was a whore," Fix tossed off.

"One thing you can bet on," said Tucker. "They didn't set out to raise no bad men."

"Boo hoo."

Tucker shot the others a circumspect glance. "You boys don't find it peculiar them bandits, cannibals, whatever they was, just let us walk out of there with all that silver?"

The big Swede laughed a little too loud, in a drunken glow. "Lucky is what we is."

"Irregular is what it is," growled Tucker. "Too good to be true. And what's too good to be true usually ain't."

Fix gripped the saddle with his knees and whapped his palomino on the haunches with his reins clenched in a black leather gloved fist so as to speed it up over the rocks. "They could have killed us right there, if they wanted to."

"But they didn't," said Bodie.

Tucker nodded, like that proved his point. "Irregular I say. Maybe they're just toying with us and this ain't over yet."

Fix looked up at the coloring sky. "Well, sun's going down, boys. Figure we best make camp."

They rode into the deep crevices of the brutal canyon country. There was an eerie atmosphere in the air, a hanging ground mist. The box canyons shadowed purple as dusk descended, the sun lowered in the sky and a dull haze settled in the area. Tucker, Fix and Bodie rode slowly through the towering chasms of crags and ravines rising up on all sides.

"I'll be glad tomorrow when we're a day's ride from here. This is a bad place," said Tucker. The gloom was dank and cold. He shivered.

Bodie reacted abruptly. "Did you hear something?"

Fix went stone still, the lean little gunfighter on high alert, braced for action. His gloved hands hovered itchy by his gunstocks in his belt. He spat a chaw of tobacco on the ground, flinty observant eyes surgically carving a line across the rocks above them. "Shhh."

Tucker unsnapped the clasp holding his Sharps rifle on his saddlebag of his dun colored stallion with a little *click*. Bodie eyeballed the others, and they caught his gaze. He snicked his glance to the left. There was a blur of movement on a scree behind him. Then they saw Calderon as he stepped out from behind a big rock a few feet ahead, holding a rifle in his bandito rags. His eyes were shiny black marbles.

"We meet up again, gringos."

The three gunfighters faced the outnumbered Mexican, sitting laconically in their saddles and cradling their weapons. The silver in the saddlebags glittered and glinted in the pale ghost of the full moon appearing overhead in the twilight sky.

Tucker's tone was blunt. "What do you want?"

Calderon nodded. "I come for the silver." They watched him. "Mostly."

Bodie got riled. "Your Jefe said we could take it."

"Jefe change his mind, gringos, and he wants his silver back."

Tucker casually scanned the visibly empty box canyon, satisfied that there were no other bandits, and then returned his gaze to the interloper who faced them with a notable lack of concern being all by himself. "You come alone," he said.

"*Solamente.*"

"So what if we don't want to give it back?"

The bandit tilted his head, the way a dog regards a kill. "I take it anyway."

Fix tickled his pearl-handled Colts with his gloved fingertips. "I'm gonna put one in his bone box just for shits and giggles."

Three against one.

Those odds might not be in their favor, Tucker reflected. All of them remembered the bullet-ridden Mosca back in Santa Sangre with one between the eyes and five in the chest standing there laughing, completely unharmed. This one could be just as indestructible. They reckoned they were about to find out. As if to make the point, a mangy buzzard alighted on a crag of granite overhead, giving those below its malignant full attention.

Tucker suppressed a smile. "So we give you the silver, and you here all by your lonesome against us three, is gonna let us live?"

Calderon seemed taken aback. "No, gringo, I am going to kill you too."

Tucker nodded. "Let's get to it then." With that, he fired both guns two-handed at point-blank range into Calderon's chest, blowing smoking bullet holes through his front, some which punched out fist-sized exit wounds in back.

The bandit staggered, but remained standing.

"Sonufabitch!" yelled Fix, flabbergasted. "Who the hell are these guys?"

Calderon spat a bloody, crumpled slug with powerful force and deadly accuracy between Tucker's eyes, breaking the flesh and hurting him.

"Ow!" The cowboy recoiled, grabbing his forehead.

By then Bodie and Fix had their guns drawn and were fanning and firing, creating clouds of smoke and muzzle flash into which the bandit disappeared from view as his body was hammered again and again with lead, apparently riddling him with bullets and blowing him to pieces. The *thunderbooms* of the gunfire echoed around the box canyons long after the shooting ceased. The smoke cleared. Calderon was gone, fled into the ravine. He was quickly glimpsed scrambling up the rocks of the chasm, lizard quick. His chortling laughter reverberated.

"We had him dead to rights! You saw!" Bodie cried, utterly rattled. He and Fix reined their horses around, swung out of the saddles and tethered the reins to a small tree. Guns drawn, the two shootists ducked into the high canyon in pursuit of Calderon.

Fix yelled back at Tucker, spraying tobacco juice. "Cover the area and keep a lookout for other'n!"

"Will do!" Tucker shouted. Staying in his saddle, clenching a big iron in each fist, he reloaded, guarding the base of the cliffs and nursing the nasty bleeding cut between his eyes.

Fix took cover behind a slab of rock and leapt around shooting a single pistol round at the bandit a hundred feet up in the chasm, who fired back. Both bullets missed and rebounded off the rocks. The ricochet of the slug exploded by Fix's head, nearly killing him as it chinked the granite.

"Shit!" he yowled.

Bodie sprang forward, firing his Winchester repeater rifle twice up at the fearsomely elusive Calderon, then ducked around behind a boulder for cover as three more bullets came from above and ricocheted deafeningly. A new threat. Five loose bullets were zigzagging out of control around the narrow cranny of the ravine. Unpredictable in their lethal trajectories, buzzing like mad bees, the rebounding slugs slammed again and again into the rocks by Fix and Bodie, making them leap like Mexican jumping beans. Impact meant instant death.

BLAM!

BLAM!

PTOW!

Fix winced and dodged up to the next rock outcropping, getting off a shot at Calderon, who buckled and grunted. His shadow was visible on the rock wall above, as the wounded bandit huddled in a cranny.

The full moon lifted in the sky.

Fix saw the long shadow of the man just over the incline, crouching in the precipice in the hard white moonlight. A groan of pain came from the figure as the moon cracked over the horizon.

"I got him, boys, you hear me? I hit him and I can hear him squealin'!" Fix yelled over his shoulder. Then the small cowboy yelled up into the depths of the canyon. "Give up fool, I know you can hear me! Don't want to kill you none after you bein' so generous with the silver so throw down yer guns and I'll let you limp outta here if ya still can!"

The sounds of anguish intensified and the silhouette of the man on the rocks above became distorted on the ravine rock wall. The shadows of the legs lengthened. The torso's shadow spasmed and seizured as the rib cage began to concave. The outline of the digits of the hands and feet extended into talons in the moonlight. Finally, the profile of its head punched out its snout into a canine skull formation with a horrific bone-snapping *crunch* that echoed through the ravine.

Fix fingered the trigger of his handgun, watching the bizarre shape shifting of the shadow.

"What the hell. . .?"

The human screams of pain gradually subsided into a rumbling growl that increased in timbre, mean and guttural, echoing through the innards of the chasm. The shadow disappeared before Fix's disturbed eyes, leaping away with supernatural speed and stealth.

A hundred yards away, Tucker sat on his horse, twin pistols gripped in his fists, knees clinging to the saddle, eyes moving back and forth as he rode this way and that through the canyon base. The horse started to freak, eyes widening big as saucers, sweat frothing on its mane. The cowboy went into high alert, searching the rugged cliff walls above and around him. Something very hungry and bloodthirsty watched him from above, then leapt an impossible distance to the ledge of the opposite stone face to observe him from another predatory vantage. Hearing gravel crumble, Tucker looked up quickly, thumbing back the hammer of his guns, as a few pebbles tumbled onto the ground by his horse's hooves. His stallion was very nervous. Tucker reacted to the fleeting silhouette darting above him, then down below. It was a great big shadow like moving black paint. Whatever was stalking him ducked into position, the hot blood pounding in its ears.

The monster pounced.

Tucker gasped.

The hairy beast stood eight feet tall with red eyes and a savage feral expression. The long snout stretched cavernously wide, exposing jagged rows of yellow fangs strung with foul saliva. Its legs and haunches were dog-like, and its talons were big as pitchforks.

"Bless my balls," Tucker choked.

The huge four-legged wolfman leapt up from a coiled crouch, big as Tucker's horse, and tackled the stallion. The steed managed to stay upright from the first punishing blow, rearing in naked terror onto its hind legs. Tucker, horrified and awe-struck to be face to face with such a creature, struggled to control his animal. Thinking fast, he reined his rearing horse and used its pawing front hooves to knock the monster back. The werewolf got piledriver-kicked in the chest and with a hideous spitting snarl went sprawling to the ground in a cloud of dust, frothing saliva, radiating insanity from its eyeballs. Frighteningly fast, the beast was instantly back up on four paws on the ground. In a swipe of its ugly claws, the monster sheared the head of the stallion clean off its thick neck in an explosion of blood and trailing meat, sinew and spinal column. The severed horse's head bounced off the rocks, bursting like a ripe watermelon. Tucker went down with it and got pinned under the saddle as the heavy steed came to earth, bridle in the gaping mouth several yards away. The saddlebags of silver spilled from the harness and dozens of gleaming metallic objects clattered and clanked against the rocks. The cowboy was trapped under his headless horse, leg stuck beneath the saddle. He opened fire with both pistols over his dead animal's flanks, shooting the fast approaching wolfman in the chest and face multiple times. The .45 caliber slugs hammered the creature back and it raged in protest, but the bullets did it no permanent damage. Tucker knew his number was up. His hammers clicked on empty chambers.

The werewolf licked its wounds, ragged holes in its fur. Its pained eyes lost their dimness as they refocused on the helpless man trapped under the decapitated horse, gaze turning bloodthirsty as it rushed him. With a mighty heave, the gunfighter hauled his leg free of the bulky saddle and limp torso of his dead steed. He rolled away in the slippery, spreading lake of blood and gore dripping from the severed neck and staggered to his feet. Quickly reloading, he faced down the snarling, rearing creature that approached him in a mountain of furred fury, distended fanged muzzle drooling. Tucker cried out to the others, true alarm in his voice. "Hey I can use some help here you fucking assholes!"

"Here I come. Hot damn," Bodie roared back. His compatriot ran into the area and hoisted his shotgun, but was immediately paralyzed by the scene before him.

Now, the gunfighters surrounded the monster in the gully in a showdown triangulation, and all three were shadowed by its immense bulk. The two tethered horses were rearing against the trammels and snorting, bicycling hooves pawing the air and kicking up clouds of dust debris in their panic. Bodie pumped his Winchester 1897 shotgun and brought it to his shoulder, drawing a bead on the creature's face.

It spun to regard him with swirling mad whirlpools of eyes. The beast's lower jaw descended and disengaged and the maw gaped, impossibly wide open.

Bodie pulled the trigger, the stock bucking against his shoulder. He pumped and fired twice more for good measure.

And blew the werewolf's head clean off.

It grew back, but messier and disfigured, like a smeared oil painting.

The huge full moon illuminated her whole ghastly tableau bright as a searchlight, as if to make sure they saw everything, sparing them nothing. The three gunfighters just stood on three sides of the beast emptying their guns into it.

The creature hissed and spat and twisted from the onslaught of lead as they drew new weapons and used those, but it grew accustomed to the bullets and dropped to all fours waiting them out until they were empty. It eyeballed them patiently until the hammers of their weapons fell on empty chambers.

Fix grabbed the silver scepter from the tabernacle as the werewolf leapt on top of him. The creature impaled itself through the left rib cage on the sterling silver spear. The point went straight through its heart and exploded out its hairy back, trailing gore. Fix's eyes widened, knowing he was dead. But he wasn't.

The wolfman was.

The monster threw back its fang-snouted head in a dying howl of dismay. Its eyes darkened, and its hideous physiognomy shuddered and went limp as it died on the spear run through its body.

Fix sucked wind.

The other two gunfighters approached. Before their very eyes, the werewolf transformed back to a man in the pale moonlight. Now mortal, the corpse was covered with bullet scars, the shotgun-shattered, disfigured head and skull in human form not grown back properly. Even so, they all recognized Calderon.

Fix leapt back in abject disgust from the naked man flopping on him, repulsed.

Tucker stared, delirious. "Grab the silver. We're getting out of here before more of those things come after us." Too shaken to speak, the gunslingers scooped handfuls of the fallen silver back into the saddle-bags. "Bodie, I'm taking your horse and you can ride with me until we can find a fresh mount."

"I didn't lose my horse, Tucker, you did. Why is it you're taking my horse?"

"Bodie, don't give me any shit. I mean right now, really don't give me any shit or I swear I will beat you down."

"Hey idiots."

Tucker and Bodie looked where Fix was pointing.

Calderon's horse calmly grazed nearby.

"Come on boys, we'll argue about this later. Let's get the fuck out of here."

The three of them swung into the saddles of the three spooked horses and galloped off into the beckoning desert.

They didn't even bother to retrieve all the spilled silver.

It was true.

Every damn word Pilar had said.

That bandit had turned into a monster man-wolf right before their eyes. They all saw it, and their guns couldn't kill it. Just the silver killed it, when stabbed through the creature's heart. Exactly like the girl had said. Damn. They should have known back at the church. He'd fired a pistolful of .45's into the bandit leader and the man *still* walked and *still* they hadn't believed her about the werewolves and the silver. But back at the box canyon, they saw the wolfman with their own eyes and *now* they believed. Damn it all to Hell. What the girl had told them all along had been the gospel truth, but they laughed her off, stole her and her people's salvation and literally threw them to the wolves. Tucker cursed himself because Pilar was truthful, had been from the moment they met, and she'd been right about everything. Everything but them being good men. She had been so wrong about that.

All three of them were lower than those monsters. Reason was they lied. They gave their word to a woman and her people, and they broke it. Mosca, he didn't lie. He was what he was and said so. In his unspeakable way, he had principles like Pilar. And the Jefe spoke the truth when he stated that Tucker, Fix and Bodie were just like he and his fellow devils. Tucker feared he'd been right when those words were uttered, his own eyes locked to Mosca's powerful perceptive stare, and it frightened him because he hadn't wanted to believe it, because what surrounded those bandits in the church were death and blood and the stench of the dying. That place was Hell, and Mosca said it was where they all belonged together. But the Jefe was right, he saw that now. Tucker, Bodie and Fix were just like them and rightly should have joined up. Only difference was they didn't have the guts to admit what they were.

The gunfighters rode hard into the night and were far away from that terrible place, but by them taking the silver, Pilar would be raped and eaten alive in the church of Santa Sangre.

Tucker knew then they could never spend the silver.

It was bad money.

They were scum.

A voice roared in his brain louder than the thunder of their galloping hooves.

No.

He and his boys were not like those dirty miserable creatures. Mosca was wrong. Tucker would prove him wrong. The cowboys were men. They had a choice. The landscape lay under the blanket of night beneath the light of the bright full moon, a patiently watchful eye waiting to see what their next move would be. Tucker suddenly reined his horse.

"Wait," he stated flatly.

The others stopped and faced him in their saddles.

"What are you doing?" Fix asked incredulously. He was gasping and sweating.

"We gotta go back." Tucker stated it like a plain and simple fact.

Bodie was beside himself. "You nuts? Back where those monsters are? We got the silver. We got all! We're rich!"

Tucker was resolved in himself. "I'm done doing the wrong thing."

Fix shook, full of dread. "We can't kill whatever those are."

"Silver bullets can."

"Give me one damn reason we should go back!" Bodie yelled.

Tucker locked his friends in a steely gaze. "Those people. We owe 'em. Gave 'em our word. We can't let those werewolves murder them people like that. If we ride away now with their silver, we'll never live it down and we'll be nothing ever again. I'm sick of things I've done, boys. It's time to stand up. I want to make a difference for a change."

Bodie looked wildly at Fix. "You ain't with Tucker on this are you?"

Fix's eyes hardened with resolve. "Tucker's right about one thing, them sons of bitches back there got to go."

That previous day, Pilar had waited patiently for the gunfighters on the other side of the ridge where they were to regroup by the blacksmith's shop if the men had lived to get the silver. The Mexican girl had heard the gunshots and knew the hour was nigh, but when she saw the three riders gallop away from the church on the horizon and keep riding north, her heart sank. They were leaving. Sunlight glinted off silver in their saddlebags and she knew the men had the treasure and were taking it. They had stolen her peoples' only protection and salvation, and she and her family were doomed. *So this is how it ends*, thought the peasant. What had she expected with such men? They were no-account gunfighters and killers no different than the evil ones who had taken her people and her church.

That was yesterday.

This afternoon, Pilar dropped to her knees and gripped her crucifix and prayed. She prayed for her people. She prayed for her sister. She prayed for their passage from this world to Heaven. She felt herself of dust and nothingness and in her wretchedness she huddled in the utter emptiness of the desert where all was weakness and brutality and ugliness and death, but she was a simple girl, and under the hot sun in the dark hour of her abandonment and despair, her faith filled her. Her prayer was simple.

Deliver Us From Evil.

Then as she opened her eyes and cast a hopeless glance into the horizon, the Mexican rose to her feet, unable to believe her eyes.

The figures of the three riders were riding toward her.

CHAPTER TEN

"**I** KNEW YOU WOULD NOT FORSAKE US, *SEÑORS.*"

The three gunfighters pulled up their horses beside her on the ridge, out of sight of the church. Tucker dismounted first. "Aw, heck. We're all gonna get killed but we're gonna take some of those sons of bitches with us."

Pilar embraced him.

The sun sank low.

He disengaged himself from the girl and tossed the saddlebags to the ground and the silver spilled out. "If we're gonna melt this into bullets we better get busy, we got two hours' daylight at best."

Fix sternly kept his own counsel as he untied his treasure-filled satchels and unloaded them onto the dirt, avoiding eye contact with the girl. Bodie stepped out of his stirrups, stinging. "But first, this little lady got some explaining to do about these sumbitches we're going up against."

Pilar eyed them all and came to a decision. "Come."

"Where?"

"With me."

The gunfighters exchanged glances, and Tucker threw a worried glance up to the sky and setting sun. Fix checked the pocket watch dangling by the chain on his vest and shook his head pessimistically, but the girl was already walking so they followed. She led them a short distance down the hard pack trail leading to the blacksmith's shed. Granite walls rose tightly on either side and midway down the path she stopped and turned to them and that's when they noticed a small cave in the arroyo. It was a few feet in height, just big enough to duck into. There was a wooden branch lying on the ground outside it. Pilar lifted it and struck a match, setting the end on fire.

Watching their heads, the gunfighters followed her in the cave.

Inside, all was darkness, but as the torch caught and the crackling flame on the branch bloomed with a gentle *hiss*, their eyes grew accustomed, and they saw glimmering faces of rock in the jumping shadows. It was cool in the cave, a relief from the heat outside. The air smelt moist, wet and earthen. They heard the clump of their boots and the *whoosh* of the flame echoing in the confines of the cavern. The faces of the three gunslingers and the peasant girl were framed in the spooky flickering glimmer of the torch in her hand. The gunslingers followed in single file behind the silhouetted back of the peasant, careful where they placed their feet as she ventured deeply into the grotto without a word. The air grew cooler, and the light from the opening disappeared behind them. After thirty paces, the girl stopped, as did the cowboys.

She held the fire up to the stone wall and they saw the primitive cave drawings. "These were made by the Old Ones," she stated with a hushed awe. "They told how men came to walk like wolves." Flames danced around a crude etching of a group of stick-figure people and their animals.

"They were beggars . . ."

Tell the tale, Pilar.

Tell it well, as your mother told you and your grandmother told her, as parents have passed the tale down from generation to generation from the olden days before our village began.

The gunfighters have now seen with their own eyes.

They must know how the werewolves came to be.

They must know who their enemy is.

Mexico badlands. Ancient times. It was hundreds of years ago before the Spaniards came, before Christ, before guns, back when the tribes lived in caves.

Nobody knew exactly where they came from.

The nomads were without a place, without a home. They had been wandering in the desert for as long as any of them could remember, and the desolation had cooked their brains. Some said they were Oaxaca Indians, whose forefathers were Aztecs. Most agree they had traveled from the south. It had certainly been a great distance. Perhaps they were driven out of their homeland by famine or plague or other tribes. Some said they were from Veracruz or Nicaragua, but they may have been Mexican. It did not matter for they had no home. They were refugees and displaced, the nameless. These homeless Indians traveled in a band of men, women and children, wearing rags, pulling carts. They were starving, dying of thirst, suffering from exposure. The group of itinerant natives drove several crude wooden carts and burros over the brutal rocky terrain under the blazing sun. They were filthy and stinking, their starving wives and children stumbling with them.

Coyotes and buzzards trailed them, waiting for the unfortunates to die.

Many dropped where they walked. The heat was as bad at night as it was in the day, boiling their brains in their skulls like ovens, their insides melting, and bodies stanching. Their skin turned black under the hot sun and eyes turned red and their tongues swelled under the heat. They fell to be abandoned to the trailing coyotes and buzzards. Without water, they sought nourishment in the saguaro and cholla cactus but the plants gave up no moisture, and they bled precious fluid from the prick of the spines. Finally, they drank their own piss, and Mosca himself pissed in the mouths of his men to try and get them a few more paces. So it is for some in the desert. But then their piss ran black and they could not drink it.

Yes, they are the same ones as the bandits in the church.

The legend tells of them on the drawings on these walls, and this is how we know it is true.

The leader of the nomads was the one who is now called Mosca, the Emperor of the Flies. He led the nomads then as he leads the bandits now, for the ones who occupy the church of Santa Sangre are the ones who staggered back then across the old lands. We know this from his ageless eyes and in them we recognize the man who was in ancient times little more than a skeleton from starvation, who is now fat from gluttony on the flesh of humans, no longer hungry and dying of thirst. Yes, we know Mosca from his eyes, the compassion gone from his gaze, but while we fear him, we understand what changed him from the terrible tale of his people, how he and his monsters came to be.

Once they were simply hungry, thirsty, yearning for a home and some small charity, but they were showed no mercy by mother earth or by the heavens, brother and sister sun and moon. The moon is a trickster, just like the coyotes, her minions on earth. We know why The Men Who Walk Like Wolves are savage as they are now, and what made them that way those long centuries ago.

Staggering through the sands under the beat of the sun, Mosca saw his ragged caravan stumbling behind him, delirious and dying, their feet crunching and sliding in the sand that burned their naked shoeless feet into blisters and sores. They trudged on from nowhere to no place. The people whimpered, the babies bawled. Their cries echoed across the desolation that mocked them by its silence. Mosca probably cast many a sunburnt, fearful glance into the feral gaze of a predatory coyote in the distance. He no doubt shivered under the scavenger's unblinking stare, for once, he knew nothing but fear. This was a weaker, broken version of the man you see now.

Perhaps it was one of the beggar women, clutching her baby to an empty teat, who pointed at a village in the distance. It was a Mexican silver town. A settlement of pueblos. They were saved. These people would surely give them food, water, take them in. Surely they could spare a few crumbs. The nomads moved their caravan down the street of the prosperous mining village. The dwellings were adobe and built into the caves on the sides of a cliff. The beggars had come upon a town that was very rich with silver. A stream ran through the village, and the indigenous local tribesmen panned for the glittering treasure. They had long hair and wore colorful headdresses and loin cloths. Piles of the valuable mineral sat by the banks. Kiosks and trading posts were set up draped with sterling silver jewelry and refined silver rocks.

Silver shined in the eyes of the beggars, who became intoxicated by all the wealth.

They ignored the fierce, repelled looks they were getting from the well-to-do townsmen. Everywhere, the despised beggars were repulsed and turned away. Huge tables of food were set up and every manner of fish, game and vegetable were laden there for a feast. The starving itinerants came to the table and with pathetic gestures begged the local merchants for scraps. They should have been fed, been given drink. The children at least. Instead, they were cast out. A heavily armed group of local men approached menacingly, lifting rocks, spears, and bows and arrows. Back the refugees were driven into Mexican badlands. The local silver village tribesmen chased the beggars into the barren foothills, tossing rocks and stoning them, and shooting at the nameless ones with arrows. The people of the silver town had much silver to spare, but no pity for the unfortunates, and they ran them off with no mercy. The desperate nomads were weeping and crying out in terror and despair as they fled with their burros and carts, or what remained of them. The men clutched their malnourished babes in their arms and embraced their sobbing wives, unable to protect them from the sticks and rocks.

Ah, see, Pilar, the gunfighters pay close heed, their eyes wide as ours were when our Old Ones told us the terrible tale, in the years before The Men Who Walk Like Wolves came. We have always expected them.

I move the billowing fiery torch to a second cave drawing beside the first, showing the stick figures throwing rocks and shooting arrows at primitive scrawl renderings of the fleeing beggars, and I continue my tale as it was told to me handed down from generations before. Now the gunfighters are exchanging glances, transfixed by the magical tale of how the werewolves came to be. I illuminate a third etching of a group of stick figures, a coyote and a big moon above them. And I continue my account . . .

That terrible night, the beggars understood it would be their last and they would starve or be eaten by coyotes. Night embraced the Mexican badlands of ancient times under the all-seeing eye of the full moon. It was an ugly white eye that never blinked, that sometimes squinted, sometimes was open, but once a month was wide as a stare and just such a yellow full moon hung overhead. The wretched nomads huddled around a campfire, half-naked with bones sticking out from malnutrition. Outside the meager warmth of their campfire, through the flames, they saw the faces of the hungry coyotes, waiting for the first chance to gobble them up. Beyond the circle of fire, past the flames, circled the scavenger silhouettes and reflective saucer eyes, fangs bared, mouths drooling. The people's dying eyes were full of fear in the firelight as they gathered together. The beggar leader Mosca grabbed their elder medicine man by the necklaces of feathers and claws and he must have gestured wildly to him, speaking in tongues. Do something. Anything. No matter what for nothing matters now, nothing could be any worse, we are at the end. And so it was young

Mosca, the leader of the beggars and Emperor of the Flies, commanded their shaman to pray to the spirits to give them powers, the strengths of the coyotes and wolves, that that they might survive the night and take what they needed to feed and protect their families.

The medicine man shook his head, pointing upward. No, he warned. Only the moon could grant those powers and the moon was a trickster, the cruel queen of the night, and she would only make things worse.

How could anything be worse, Mosca insisted. He punched the beggar elder and knocked him down, drawing his knife. Behind him, all the people yelled at the old man as the coyotes closed in. I can hear them now and were I in their position would have done the same. The nomads warned the medicine man to use his magic or they would die and prom-ised to throw him to the wolves first if he did not. Reluctantly, the shaman rose to his feet and began to chant, throwing powders and turning his head to the giant orb of the full moon above. All the people chanted and danced. Outside the glimmering perimeter of the campfire, the shadows of the dancing beggars became distorted, grew giant and strange, and the coyotes fled in yelping terror.

They prayed to the moon to become as wolves, and the moon she answered their prayers.

Speechless, the cowboys watch as I move the torch to a fourth cave drawing. It shows a large number of stick figures with their arms, legs and heads pulled to pieces over a red swath. Crude but scary sketches of wolflike creatures with red mouths and eyes and long teeth and claws are pictured ripping them asunder. I continue . . .

The first werewolves attacked the village that had refused them food and they devoured everyone and had full bellies. The Mexican silver town of olden times was a slaughterhouse. By the stark light of the full moon, a savage and hungry pack of wolfmen tore the villagers limb from the limb as the ground ran black with meat and blood and they gobbled screaming children whole. It was a ghastly spectacle. And after they butchered and ate the people, they took the precious silver. One of the creatures, Mosca it is said, grabbed clawfuls of moon-drenched silver jewelry from a shattered kiosk in its paws and stared mad-eyed at the shimmering metal, its slavering jaws drooling with greed. By the time The Men Who Walk Like Wolves departed, not a living soul in the village remained.

It is then that the truly terrible part of the legend begins.

The sky of ancient times lightened overhead.

Sunup.

The moon gave up her domain to rest, for she had been very busy and was tired, and her single eye closed. After their feast, the werewolves returned to their wives and children and the moon laughed cruelly before she departed. The nomad camp was quiet. The beggar leader Mosca, returned to naked human form, stirred awake. He blinked open his eyes in the harsh sun, and saw the ground soaking wet. Red. The same sticky red smearing his hands he regarded in growing horror, the same red filling his mouth he rubbed. Removing the piles of silver treasure he lay covered with, Mosca sat up and saw why everything was so very damp.

The tiny, scattered gnawed bones of his devoured child were beside him.

Right next to the severed breast and upper section of his half-eaten wife.

And the beggar screamed in unimaginable horror and beheld all the other nomad men returned to human form standing and screaming and staggering in indescribable terror amidst the chewed remains of their families.

For the moon was a trickster and made The Men Who Walk Like Wolves eat their own. For by giving up their human nature, she had made them base and vile below all other beasts, forever outcast, cursed to become the monsters every full moon.

As a coyote in the distance threw its head back and howled, the hideous screams of the beggar men who had been driven mad echoed like a death rattle across the barren land.

So it is said this is how the werewolves came to be.

And that is the end of my story.

Finished, Pilar regarded the attentive faces of the gunfighters standing by the cave painting, rugged countenances glimmering grimly by the flickering torchlight in the darkness. It took a few moments while the cowboys digested the legend before any of them spoke and that was after they looked one another over and up and down and back again.

"S'pose that's as good an explanation as any," Tucker said.

"Wouldn't have believed it if we hadn't seen these things with our own eyes. It's why we came back," Fix added.

"I almost feel sorry for them poor sorry ass sons of bitches." Bodie shook his head.

"Puts me of a mind to put 'em out of their misery."

"So the silver, the moon cursed that too, made it what would kill them?"

"*Si*. Or release them."

"That can be arranged."

"Little lady," Fix said quietly. "Guessin' by whoever drawed them pictures, the silver town stood in the valley where your village sits now, don't it?"

She nodded. "And the werewolves have returned. As they have returned before. And will again."

The little gunfighter scratched his jaw. "Well, I best believe we need to do something about that. That just won't do."

☾

The pale ramparts of the pueblo church and steeple of Santa Sangre up on the hill lorded forebodingly over the huddled huts of the deserted village down below gripped by fingers of lengthening late afternoon shadows. The dwindling sun festered in the inflamed sky, lowering relentlessly toward the horizon. The vague outline of the nearly full moon intruded belligerently in the atmosphere, a ghostly specter impatient for the departure of the sun. There was a hush over the land.

Across the valley, the blacksmith's shop plumed smoke into the dusky sky.

Inside, the four worked.

Two huge weathered cast iron kettles were set on blazing coals and logs. A wooden cask of frigid river water sat a few feet from that, the top lidless.

Bodie dumped the saddlebags of sterling silver, religious artifact chalices, statuettes, plates and crucifixes into the pots. The silver figures lost their shape as they melted into a shiny, bubbling soup.

The heavy molds for the bullets were set nearby.

The job would obviously have been impossible without them. There were four of the mold platters in the .45 and .50 caliber dimensions. Fortunately, the peasants built their own bullets for hunting and protection because it was cheaper than purchasing new rounds and had made careful retrieval of all their empty slug casings when they fired them. The men of the village had been trained in the frugal habit from childhood when they first went hunting with their fathers, using the old bolt action Henry rifles they kept in good repair. A cask for gunpowder sat outside, safely clear of any flames. It was one of the few purchases the villagers were required to make from the town they ventured into once a month. Alas, the barrel of gunpowder was almost empty and the gunfighters needed to be parsimonious with the powder in their own bullets. Luckily, they had those aplenty.

After emptying their rifles, pistols, cartridge belts and the pouches of ammunition in their saddlebags, Bodie had counted out 1,010 rounds to their name.

While the silver melted, Pilar stirred the pot with an iron ladle. Tucker and Fix sat in the dirt with a pair of pliers each, tugging the lead bullet heads out of brass casings from the pile they had made of their rounds heaped beside them. They used a vise clamp to hold the casings as they yanked out the rounds and dumped them in another pile. Once those were removed, they took the empty cartridge casings and set them upright side by side on a wooden plank they placed on the ground, mindful not to spill any of the precious gunpowder. They had 450 headless slugs in rows so far, awaiting the insertion of the silver heads.

It had taken an hour, working without respite or discussion, each knowing their jobs, while the sun splayed deepening crimson shadows through the wooden slats of the blacksmith's shack on its steady march to the horizon and oblivion of the day.

The close rank air smelled of steel and firewood and char and body odor. The kettles of silver bubbled and popped like gleaming chromium molten lava, casting scintillating reflections on Pilar as she circled the ladle, making her face look metallic as a statue. She nodded at Bodie, and he came over with the first bullet mold, a steel tray with fifty rounded slots in a grid. Clenching the heavy plate with both hands by a pair of tongs, the Swede held it up as the peasant girl lifted a ladle dripping with pure liquid silver from the kettle. Careful not to burn either of them with the steaming brew, she poured the silver directly into the bullet mold, round hole by round hole. Her meticulous and deliberate manner ensured there was no overflow, and they wouldn't have to scrape the mold clean, which would waste precious time. It was a process that had them as taut in concentration as if they had been unloading and setting fuses to dynamite sticks wet and volatile with nitroglycerine from the heat. The lives of the four were in just as much jeopardy. When done, she nodded, and the big man very carefully lowered the mold into the cold water of the cask where it instantly steamed and *hissed* and turned the metal solid.

Removing the mold and the silver slugs from the water cask, Bodie walked over to Tucker and Fix then swung a sledgehammer to knock the sterling bullet heads on the ground. While his compatriots gathered them up, he returned with the mold clenched in the clamps and held it out for Pilar. She began to ladle fresh molten silver from the kettle into the slots. The other two gunfighters set to work building the silver bullets directly. Putting ten empty gunpowder-filled casings at a time into the vise clamp, the men used pliers to press the new silver heads into the openings. They moved swiftly, and with the process repeated several times, the pile of magic bullets that would kill the werewolves grew on the ground.

The first set of silver bullets bad been cast.

They had fifty.

They had two hours.

Forty minutes produced five hundred fresh slug heads that Tucker and Fix completed as Pilar poured hot silver into the molds. Bodie used the tongs to dunk the hissing red hot molds into wooden buckets of cold river water. The steam cast a sinister fog over the primitive blacksmith's shop, wreathing the heroes in mythic silhouette as they did the work of the righteous. All were bathed in sweat. It was hot as a furnace in the close confines of the shed. Fix had loosed his collar, and Tucker had taken his shirt off. Bare chested, his muscles were drenched in perspiration. They passed a bottle of rotgut 100-proof whisky. This time the girl took a drink.

Tucker checked his pocket watch. "We've an hour and fifteen minutes to sundown, give or take."

Fix used a wrench to tug the slugs out of the bullet casings of their ammo belts then used the same tool to insert new sterling silver heads into the empty cartridges, careful not to spill the powder. A considerable heap of silver bullets sat on the wooden plank beside him.

"We got six hundred and seventeen rounds. We're doing about five hundred and thirty an hour. Let's pick up the pace, boys."

Tucker took inventory. "By my count, there's twenty-five of them sumbitches, less the one we sent to perdition back at the canyon."

"That's twenty-four hearts." Bodie grinned. "Right now, we got twenty-five shots apiece to nail 'em. We do our jobs right, we should be doing good on bullets."

"There's twenty-four guns between them. We're gonna get hit and we may get shot dead so it could be two of us, or just one of us, doing the killing and we can't miss," Tucker pointed out. "One or two of us goes down, it fall t'other grab the others' silver bullets and he may not be situated."

"Meaning?"

"We need more bullets."

"He's right, there's only three of us and twenty-four of them."

"There are four," Pilar corrected.

"You ain't coming," refuted Bodie.

"I can fight." The beautiful brown girl stuck out her jaw, eyes proud.

Bodie shook his head. "That Hell-hole church is going to be a slaughterhouse, and it ain't no fit place for a lady."

"They are my people. I will fight. I will die."

Bodie kept working. "There's no way that's happening."

"Maybe she has a point," Fix disagreed.

"Tuck, talk some sense into her," the Swede practically shouted.

Tucker made the final decision. "We're going to need all the guns we can. She's coming. That's it."

"Can you shoot?" Fix inquired without preamble.

The look in the beautiful peasant girl's eyes revealed telltale hesitation.

Fix sighed. "Beautiful."

Tucker got off his knees, setting down the wrench and sliding his soaked shirt over his bare, rippling, sweat-dripping chest. "Well, little girl, if you're gonna go in guns blazing, I best believe you need to learn how to pull a trigger. I'll school ya." He rose. "Fix, Bodie, you stay here and keep making the bullets, many as you can. I'm gonna take the lady a short ride away where them sumbitches can't hear the shots 'n learn her to shoot."

Fix squinted. "We ain't got the bullets to waste."

Tucker ignored that, grabbing a few fistfuls of the standard .45s and displayed them in his open palm. "With these. Can't use none of our regular ammo anyhows. I'll gather the empties and bring 'em back." Holding out his hand like a gentleman, Tucker helped Pilar to her feet, and she blushed demurely. "Back in a few."

They departed the blacksmith's shop for the tethered horses outside and rode off.

Bodie glared at the departing riders as he poured more molten silver into the molds and set the container into the cauldron of icy river water with a steaming sizzle. "He's gonna fuck her."

Fix humorlessly jammed another gleaming slug into an open cartridge casing and tweaked it in with the clamps. "Shut up and work."

Both gunfighters returned to their business of manufacturing the silver bullets.

The desert flowers were in bloom, bright yellow and red blossoms on the arms of the saguaro and cholla cacti radiant in the hillocks of the barrows. Out in the desert a mile off, the two small figures of Tucker and Pilar rode across the big empty of the badlands as the sun inched closer to the distant mountains. Behind them, the church on the hill was miles back. Tucker had been following Pilar, and the short ride had put them well out of earshot of the village as they negotiated their horses into a verdant valley by a pebble-strewn draw. The creek that ran past the blacksmith's shed had widened into the clear stream that snaked through the gully, its fresh waters giving sustenance to all manner of vegetation in the lyrical oasis. This is what they had followed. The gunfighter knew they were running out of time, but trotting behind her, the sweet smell of her drifting back at him and mixing with the fragrance of the flora inclined him to linger. This was true beauty, and he had seen too little of it over the grim horrors of the last twenty-four hours. He just wanted to dawdle and take pleasure from it. Perhaps if they survived the coming battle, he could spend a little more time here. Tucker felt renewed, like he had something to live for. Best of all, it was just him and her. A man might stay awhile. A towering mescal cactus dominated the rocky, stark open area. That's what he had been looking for.

The cowboy reined his horse. "This'll do."

He dismounted and helped Pilar from her mustang, then started tying off their horses by the shore of the creek in the overhand of a paloverde tree. The steeds immediately stuck their snouts in the cool burbling brook and became otherwise occupied quenching their thirst.

The peasant waited patiently as the shootist unloaded an ammo belt from his saddlebags.

"We'll use yonder cactus for target practice," he said.

Pilar watched Tucker with big moist brown eyes, taking him in and absorbing every word he said. A soft wind whipped up over the plains and wafted her baggy clothes around the pleasing swells of her body. She brushed dust from her face.

Tucker drew a Colt Peacemaker and flipped open the cylinder to reveal a half-empty gun.

"You open a gun like this. That button there."

She nodded, paying close attention.

"Take yer bullets, round side down, and stick 'em in the holes." He loaded the gun. Pressed the cylinder back into the revolver. "Close it till it clicks and yer good t' go."

Pilar smiled, standing beside him.

He lengthened his arm, lined up a shot on the cactus a hundred yards away and squeezed off a shot.

The blast reverberated around the valley, scattering crows and a nervous lizard that ducked under a rock.

Pilar shook at the sound.

A chunk of splintered plant fell from the dead center of the cactus.

"Easy as milking a cow, see?"

"Let me try," Pilar said eagerly.

"Your turn, m'am." He placed the gun in her hand and their fingers touched, lingering. When he let go, the weight of the gun dropped her hand to her side from the heft.

"It's so big and heavy," she gasped.

"Mebbe it's best you use both hands, so grip it tight with both paws round the handle, and, you're right handed so it seems, put your right finger around the trigger." Fueled with adrenaline, the lovely peasant girl hoisted the pistol straight-armed with both hands and pointed it at the mescal cactus target.

"Take careful aim," he instructed. The gunslinger positioned himself behind her and ran his big, scarred hands down her elbows, peering over her shoulder. He smelled her hair and tried to focus, adjusting her arms to point the gun at the distant mescal. "Good. Now. Use one eye and look down the twin notches on the back of the gun and line 'em up with the sight notch on the front of the barrel so they are one thing, and put that on your target."

"Yes."

"You got 'em lined up?"

"Yes."

"Now, nice 'n easy, squeeze the trigger, don't pull. Go."

She fired with a satisfying *crack-boom,* and the heavy hog leg kicked like a mule, knocking her backward into his big body, which he didn't mind, making him chuckle. Fear flashed in her eyes from the smoking iron she nearly dropped when it went off. The bullet ricocheted off a distant rock, missing the cactus.

"Try again. This time use your wrists to take the impact, now squeeze the trigger, nice 'n slow, don't pull. And if y'need a little motivation, picture that tree is one of them wolfmen sumbitches."

Swallowing, Pilar gamely took two-handed aim again with the Colt revolver at the cactus, carefully peering down the sight and this time she did it right. Squeezing the trigger, she blasted a hole in the trunk, dead center, flinching from the recoil but keeping her grip on the gun.

A tine flew to perdition.

"Good!"

The peasant girl fired twice, putting two more rounds into the plant, a quick study.

"Good girl."

She smiled proudly and slid back in his arms as she lowered the pistol, slowly turning as she slipped the gun back in his holster, hands traveling up his shoulders as she stared in his eyes.

And they kissed.

His hands moved under her shirt. "Beauty like you a man'd walk into Hell for." His fingers got a handful of smooth tit and hard nipple. Pilar leaned back her head and her lips turned rubber with arousal.

"Burn with me," she pleaded, guttural and lustful.

She dropped the loose outfit from her shoulders and stood naked in front of him. Her proud breasts were nut brown, high and firm with dark nipples flushed with health. Her buttocks swelled in twin supple mounds. Her legs were long and strong, to the bushy black triangle below her navel. Tucker thought in her unbridled nakedness she was the most beautiful woman he had ever laid eyes on, and he knew for certain what he was fighting for and why he had come.

Tucker stripped down and Pilar took in the fullness of him with a gasp, her breath catching. Then he kissed her hard, filling her lungs.

He eased her onto the ground.

The girl's legs parted, knees in the air, and the cowboy pressed himself in and she cried out as he came up against a stubborn resistance inside her. She gripped his shoulders, bearing up bravely as with new gentleness he pushed slowly and persistently until her girlhood gave way and he was slowly thrusting as she wept on his shoulder and a torrent of tender obscenities escaped her lips. They made vigorous love in the dirt until they came hard and loud and fell in each other's arms, still joined deep inside the sweet warm clench of her. They lay that way under the watchful desert flowers, naked bodies intertwined, and he saw the drops of blood on her smooth thigh. It was with the greatest reluctance that he disengaged of her and both nude lovers rose to their feet, walked into the cold stream and bathed one another tenderly head to foot.

The sun's descent called them back to town.

Tucker stood buckling his chaps while Pilar dressed in her baggy garb, drying herself from the creek and brushing her hair with her hands. The girl was flushed with physical satisfaction and a private, secret pleasure in her eyes. He watched her in all her mysteriousness, feeling young again, like he used to be. It had been so long. There were a few drops of blood on her pants. "We better go," she said.

"Reckon we best."

They mounted up.

As they settled into their saddles, he looked at her. "Pilar . . ."

She pushed her hair back from her happy face with her hands and gave him a well-laid smile. "Yes, Tucker," she said, her face and voice womanly now.

"I was your first." His voice was tender and awkward. She beamed at him and nodded. "A girl as beautiful as you. A village of young men. How can that be?"

The girl spoke from her heart as she gazed into his eyes with the force of nature. "I wanted my child to be a man such as you, a hero, not peasants like the men of my town. I saved myself waiting for the day you would come and always knew that you would answer my prayers."

He tipped his hat. "Pleased to be of assistance. Let's ride."

They galloped back toward the village.

Both, in ways separate and same, now were ready.

The blacksmith's shop was wreathed in smoke and steam. The sun festered in the bottom of the sky. Fix gave it the stink eye as he drank some well water and splashed some on his face, heading back inside. They were all out of time.

Bodie melted the silver. The saddlebags of church artifacts were empty and had all been melted down by now. His companion joined him quietly pounding the silver bullet heads into open cartridges with a mallet.

The hours had passed swiftly.

The pile of bullets had grown large.

They had what they had. It would have to do.

"Where the hell are they?" Bodie wondered.

The other cowboy gave him a wry glance.

Bodie stewed. "The hell you say."

"Keep your mind on your work." Fix hammered away.

They busied making a few more silver bullets.

A short while later at dusk, the glowing Tucker and Pilar rode back to the blacksmith's shop and reentered the structure. The other cowboys flicked glances at their friend, savvying the situation. It was twilight, and they had melted down all the silver and turned it into slugs. "We have exactly 837 rounds," counted Bodie.

Fix eyeballed the dimming sky. "And daylight's a memory."

"There's something else you must know." Pilar faced them all and her eyes were urgent. "Use caution not just not to be killed. Take great care not to be bitten by the werewolf, for if you are, if they draw your blood, you will become a monster such as they. This is how they make others like them."

"So we just get bit by one of these sumbitches we sprout hair?" Tucker inquired nervously.

"*Si*." She nodded.

"Good to know," said Fix.

Tucker drew his pistols, spinning them around his fingers until they were butt side up, and he flipped open the twin cylinders. "We got some killing to do."

They armed up, loading the gleaming silver rounds, pressing the cartridges into ammo belts, shoving them into the breeches of their rifles, plugging them into the orifices of every pistol they had and sticking them into the slots in their belts.

"What's that?" Tucker asked. Bodie was grinning proudly, holding out three crude but nasty sharp silver blades atop sledgehammer-rounded silver grips he had forged.

"A little something for in-close work." The Swede chuckled affably and tossed his friends the two silver blades, sheathing the third himself.

"Let's make a plan." The natural leader hunkered down in the flickering firelight of the coals, drawing with a poker a crude square map layout of the church floor plan in the dirt on the ground. "This is the chapel. Front door here."

He made an X.

"Back room where they got those people, here."

Another X.

"We're here."

X.

"Figure we got mebbe twenty-four of them sumbitches, mostly inside here." He scratched dirt with the poker head inside the scrawled rectangle. "But be careful they aren't positioned outside, anywhere around here." He drew a circle around the square. The other two cowboys and the peasant girl squatted beside him around the map, reviewing it alertly.

Fix raised an eyebrow, studying the diagram. "They got a back door to this dump?"

Pilar nodded. "Yes, a small door in the back that goes under the church to a hatch into the back room."

Bodie uncrossed his legs. "The sumbitches know about that?"

Pilar's gaze clouded with uncertainty. "I do not know."

Fix looked up, chewing his lip. "Maybe we can create a diversion in the front, and Pilar can slip past them varmints through the back."

"Good." Tucker nodded. He used his finger to draw arrows and lines indicating the four of them and their directions of attack. "So that's the plan. Fix, Bodie, you and me ride up front, go in blasting. Pilar goes around back, sneaks in and lets them folks out the back way."

Bodie shrugged, amenably. "Whatever you boys think is best."

Tucker looked them all over. "If we're lucky, the werewolves won't notice those people is on the move until it's too late."

Pilar's brow furrowed. "But what if they see us in the back and attack. We will be slaughtered."

Bodie nodded. "The girl's got a point. It's risky. Those people don't have weapons. I say we give her a few guns and silver ammo so she can pass 'em out to her people that best can shoot, that way we squeeze those creatures in a shit sandwich." Bodie looked at Pilar, and she nodded with a small smile.

"If we die, we die bad."

Fix stood up with a grunt and straightened, hands on his hips, leaning back and popping his spine and stuffing his pearl-handled Colts into his side holsters with a squeak of leather. "Then there's only one thing for us to do."

Tucker looked at him sideways, fingering his beard. "What's that?"

"*Kill 'em all.*" A slow smile spread across the hard little man's face. His eyes twinkled. The others grinned too, and just then a vast and ominous epic shadow fell across their faces as through the slats in the blacksmith's shed a mean slender red thread on the horizon was all that remained of the sun.

"It's time," said Tucker.

"Let's do it," said Bodie.

"What are we waitin' for?" said Fix.

The four heroes gathered up their ammo belts stuffed with silver bullets and their many guns. They stuck the rifles, pistols and silver rounds that were not on their person in their saddlebags and saddle holsters, weighing down their steeds. Tucker loaded up Pilar's mustang with weapons, seeing to it she had guns and ammo to distribute to her villagers when she broke them out. The animals were tense and obedient, somehow sensing the great battle ahead. Outside the blacksmith's shop, the three gunfighters and the peasant girl mounted up on their horses.

The men tipped their hats to her.

199

"Good luck." Tucker smiled.

She crossed herself. "God bless you."

The three men and the lone girl rode off in two different directions.

CHAPTER ELEVEN

THE VILLAGE LAY IN REPOSE AT DUSK.

The deserted town was bathed in an ominous red twilight hue.

Three lone gunfighters rode through the shadows of the empty square toward the hill leading up to the church. Above them dead ahead, Santa Sangre loomed, its stark white walls and steeple bathed in crimson light, the doors and windows shadowed, like a stripped skull. The hard men kept their hands near their weapons as they trotted down the empty dirt street. It was a long ride, and the world seemed to bend around them, extending the distance toward the inevitable. Nothing moved, there was no sound but the quiet clop of their horses. The vultures were gone, resting up for the feast to come. It was easy to imagine. Ever bigger grew the hill and, atop, the towering ramparts of the brooding mission of iniquity where their combined intertwined destinies had led them. Then the town fell behind them and their horses embarked upon the gravel path winding up a steep grade toward the gloomy doors of perdition, and the hour was nigh.

The untended fields sprawled eerily quiet and still in the gloaming. Dead crops were draped in burgeoning shadows. The peasant girl rode bravely alone around the back of the hill leading toward the rear of the church, steeple rising sinister and stark against the dying embers of the sun. The white pueblo of the church of Santa Sangre was the color of blood, like its namesake, she thought. The wheels of fate were set in motion and it was in the hands of God now, Pilar accepted as she gripped her reins. She knew no fear. She was doing her part.

As her rump smacked against the saddle leather, the girl scanned the arid piles of wheat and corn on either side of the rows. She remembered running through them as a little girl with flowers in her hair when the crops grew tall and proud and golden, waving to the farmers on some beautiful forgotten day when the village was happy, and she was young and knew what it was to play. Now, as Pilar rode through the decaying chaff of the fields, she beheld the exaggerated shadow of herself on her horse, rifle sticking up, bosom sticking out, hair seeming to billow and blow ethereally behind her in the wind like a warrior goddess. She thought that mythical silhouette looked as splendid as a heroine on one of the cover paintings of her dime western books. Yet it was her, so she breathed that idealized shadow image into her whole being. It buttressed her spirit and she drew strength from it. Alone on the ride to Santa Sangre, profoundly solitary in the calm before the coming storm, engulfed by the hush of vast empty fields, Pilar knew what it was to be her own hero. The hill to the cathedral was very close now, maybe a hundred yards, and the narrow trail she would ride up came into view. Many thoughts filled her young mind now. She wondered how many of her people were still alive within the walls ahead. She wondered if the gunfighters had already arrived there. Over and over in her head, she planned her entrance through the back door of the church, so she did it right when the time came, knowing that moment was mere minutes away. She must not fail. They must not fail. But a church was as good a place to die as any, Pilar thought, thinking the gunfighters' wry cynicism must be rubbing off on her.

Now the time for thinking was over.

The time for action had come.

Her horse took the hill.

The sun dropped below the bloody horizon by the time The Guns of Santa Sangre rode to the doors of the church. They were draped with ammunition belts loaded with silver bullets, and each of them carried a rifle slung over their shoulder and had two pistols stuck in their holsters.

Mosca sat on the step waiting for them, his eyes like destiny. "I said you would be back."

"Let them people go."

"And if we don't?"

"We'll kill all you son of a bitches."

The Jefe smiled ironically to himself, tossed a pebble, then rose to his feet, brushing off the seat of his pants. "You should not have brought my mother into it, gringo. My mother is not a bitch. She heard how you insulted her and she is very angry. She is here now. With us. Look." Mosca pointed to the sky and the almost full moon on the rise, an omnipresent white orb looming like a hallucination in the feverish nocturnal desert atmosphere. The gunslingers saw the moon but looked quickly back to the bandit leader, whose voice had disturbingly changed, becoming guttural and coarse. "*Mi madre ve y oye todos*, she sees and hears all. My mother, the mother of my men and I, is the moon and we are her children, *comprende*? The children of the night. *Los ninos de la noche*. She is full. I love her. *Amor a mi madre*. Tonight she shall enjoy watching as you die very, very badly, gringos."

Bodie, Fix and Tucker looked around and realized that while Mosca was talking, fifteen bandits had quietly surrounded them like prowling coyotes, closing off the road up the hill. Tall, hulking shadows lurked in the pale moonlight and their eyes seemed to be glowing red.

Mosca grinned, flashing his rows of gold teeth. He closed his mouth, smiling, working his jaw, his tongue moving inside his cheeks. Then he put his hand on his mouth and spat something into it. Reaching out his fist, he opened that hand and in his palm was a pile of gold teeth. The gunfighters looked at the bandit leader who looked back at them, his mouth opening as his lips pulled back in his fat face revealing rows of toothless gums. Then, before their eyes, new teeth pushed through the gums, sharp and white and canine.

The gunslingers exchanged laconic glances. "This is bad."

The other bandits were disrobing, their bodies convulsing.

The cowboys' frightened horses suddenly reared, neighing in raw terror, nostrils snorting, hooves pawing the air, pitching the gunfighters out of their saddles to the dirt. The force of the impact knocked the wind out of Tucker, Bodie and Fix. As they crawled to their hands and knees and looked around, what they witnessed was beyond comprehension.

Mosca and his men were going into seizures, screaming, howling and frothing at the mouth, their entire bodies spasming. Beneath their stretching skin and new thick, black hair, their bones were lengthening and rearranging with cracking, ripping, squishing sounds. Their lower legs began to bend and extend like the hind legs of dogs, kicking up the dust, which filled the air and turned them into nightmarish silhouettes. Long claws popped out their nails in splatters of blood as the spikes cut through the flesh of their fingertips. Their hands curled and elongated into foot-long talons.

Tucker grabbed for his fallen pistol that lay by the foot of one of the bandits and saw that foot sprout fur and the toes grow pads and bloat into a paw.

"Aim for the hearts!" shouted Tucker.

A barrage of bullets exploded as the gunfighters' pistols blazed away, and they pumped silver into the chests of eight of the transforming werewolves. The cowboys were dead shots and punched ragged holes into two of the beasts' rib cages over their beating hearts. Instantly, those creatures roared and howled in dying agony, dropping to the ground, huge paws and talons slashing the air until they stiffened, fell still and died in the dirt, blood jetting like fountains from their wounds.

As soon as they were dead, the werewolves instantly transformed back into men. The inhuman shapes of the monsters' awful anatomies shrunk, reverting to the small, broken, filthy naked bodies of the bandits sprawled on the ground.

Immediately, their werewolf brethren set upon the human carcasses of their comrades and ate them whole. The beasts' savage canine jaws ripped and tore flesh and muscle from bloody bone and gulped it down viciously, eyes red coals, clawing and slashing one another to get at the chow. The wolfmen were distracted in their cannibalistic feeding frenzy long enough for the gunfighters to crawl to cover for a few short moments. The cowboys tightened themselves into a circle, facing the werewolves who again closed in on all sides, shrieking and spitting in mad-eyed rage. The hairy creatures reared and crouched, glaring at the gunfighters.

They attacked.

The three horses the shootists rode in on rolled and tumbled down the hill, throwing up huge clouds of dirt, until the steeds got themselves upright and stood outside the perimeter, rearing and watching the action. Scrambling to his boots, Bodie drew both revolvers, silver bullet tips glinting in the cylinder, and stood to face the bandits. His eyes widened. The gunslinger was staring right in the furry face of Mosca, whose jawbone dislocated as the front upper teeth stretched forward, cartilage crunching. Further and further, jagged white fangs sliced through the gums like rolls of razors, as the nose became a black snout that jutted two feet out of the face to give him the head of a gigantic wolf. Hairy, pointed ears twitched. Saliva and froth spewed from the mouth as its long tongue slathered and swept hungrily. The spine stretched and bullwhipped as the rib cage became narrow and deep and hollowed, and on its huge back paws with its long arms and massive talons, the eight-foot werewolf towered over Bodie. A thick, bushy and furred tail swept behind its haunches.

Tucker, Bodie and Fix blasted away with their irons, unleashing gunshots that leapt like bolts of lightning from their muzzles as they fired into the mob of wolfmen, sending a few more straight to Hell. The moon splashed down on the scene like a searchlight, emblazoning the creatures the bandits had become. Their horrific transformation complete, fourteen of the hissing, snarling, roaring monsters clambered over one another to tear the cowboys to ribbons. The three men hit the ground and rolled on their stomachs through the open doors of the church, taking the battle into the belly of the beast that was Santa Sangre.

Inside the gloomy pueblo chapel, the gunfighters ducked behind a blood-smeared pew, emptying their guns into the wall of monsters. Tucker unslung his Winchester repeater and gave Bodie and Fix cover as they reloaded their pistols with silver rounds from the belts strapped on their chests. They were instantly surrounded as the fearsome hairy creatures advanced on them through the open doors of the church and closed in right and left through the nave like a pack of titanic wolves. The air was rent with a supernatural cacophony of throaty roars. Bodie and Fix rearmed and spun their cylinders shut with a whizzing *whirr*, a Colt pistol in each hand. The gunfighters took deadly aim at the werewolves who leaped for them just as they unleashed silver with their guns.

Pumping a shot smack into the heart of a wolfman, Fix saw it slam back into the pueblo wall and sink to the floor, smearing a snail trail of gore as it reverted to dead human form. The other creatures hungrily devoured the corpse and tore at one another to get a mouthful of a ripped-off severed leg, tugging the limb in their jaws like mongrels fighting over a bone.

Inhuman shadows fell over Bodie, who whirled to see two creatures pouncing toward him. With a gun in each hand he shot them in the hearts and it was two dead stinking bandits that landed on him before he shoved them off and fired at the other monsters over the pews. He ran out of bullets fast and was just starting to reload when he saw the shadow of a werewolf jumping at him from behind. Yanking the forged silver knife from his belt, Bodie spun and slammed the blade to the hilt in the monster's upper left chest, giving the weapon a nasty twist as he killed the beast.

The close quarters of the church rang loudly with the roars and snarls of the creatures and the deafening gun-blasts reverberating off the walls. Combined with the horrid, fetid stench of the creatures, the smell of gunpowder and cordite and their own sweat of fear, the gunfighters were nearly overcome.

One of the bullets ricocheted in a shower of sparks off a holy water fountain and the sparks quickly ignited the hanging curtains by the busted windows. A serpent of flame slithered up the drapes and coiled across the wooden beams of the ceiling, a viper's nest of fire quickly spreading over the roof.

Tucker raised his rifle to his shoulder and squeezed the trigger just as a werewolf dove on him, slavering jaws spread wide as an open bear trap. The creature landed mouth first on the long steel barrel of the Sharp's rifle and when the weapon discharged it exploded its skull in a gory raining galaxy of brain and fur and bone fragment as its head was blown clean off. The heavy carcass of the monster landed on the gunfighter, who yanked the barrel of the rifle out of the grisly trailing viscera of the blood-jetting neck stump still dangling a loosely attached lower jaw.

But the werewolf was not dead.

Its decapitated torso became violently animated, and its talons struggled to slash at the cowboy pinned under it.

Tucker pulled the trigger repeatedly but he was out of bullets, silver or otherwise. Desperately, he quickly brandished the Sharps rifle, gripping it by the stock, and the hot barrel seared his palm as he braced it against the wolfman's powerful limbs, pinning the talons away from his face the claws slashed viciously at. "Boys!" he yelled in panic. The haunches of the headless creature's hindquarters pumped, its rear legs climbing against the floor, padded back talons digging into the blood-slippery wood. Tucker struggled, his grip on the gun keeping the monster off him weakening as the jagged claws *whished* through the air by his face to claw it off. Suddenly, the cowboy felt an awful searing pain in his shoulder and winced as blood sprayed his face from a ragged wound. He was going to die for sure, he knew it, and gave a last hopeless sidelong glance at the ground to see Fix drawing one of his pistols from his holster and tossing it skidding around and around in circles, across the floor right into Tucker's open hand. That same hand closed around the handle of the Colt Peacemaker and jammed the muzzle of the long barrel under the left side of the chest of the werewolf where the heart was. His forefinger squeezed the trigger, blowing the still-pumping heart out the back of the monster's spine.

The creature fell across him, very dead.

Santa Sangre was engulfed in flames by now, and angry tendrils of conflagration plumed across the wooden rafters of the church as smoke billowed through the fulgurations of fire. Pieces of blazing timber dropped from the ceiling inferno onto a few of the werewolves and they instantly ignited, fur spewing flames, but still the burning creatures attacked.

Hell had come to earth.

The outside of the church sat under the dank cover of night beneath the bright nearly full moon. Unobserved, Pilar carefully rode her horse up to the rear hitching post, dismounted, drew her pistol she held with both hands. She slung the straps of four repeater rifles over her young shoulders, grabbing the bag of silver bullets her gunfighters had given her to arm the peasants. The girl could hear the roars and gunshots booming from within the cathedral. There was a thickening fog of smoke from the fire wreathing the area. The peasant girl drifted in silhouette, clenching the hog leg of a pistol as she slid up against the wall, eyes wide, checking the area for werewolves.

A fresh fusillade of shots from inside.

More monstrous roars.

Now screams.

The hulking shape of something huge reared in the dense smoke. Gasping, Pilar raised the gun in both hands and pointed it. She released her breath. The apparition was only another frightened horse tethered to a post. Exhaling, the peasant reached the tiny door at the base of the wall. It was a square of oak, with a latch on a dowel that slotted into a notch. She opened it and crawled inside, bravely entering the church on her hands and knees.

Under the building there was a crawlspace, barely two feet of distance between the cathedral floorboards and the dirt ground. Pulling herself along on her belly, the peasant girl gripped the guns and crawled beneath the floor over bare earth through the murky darkness. Firelight pulsed through the smoky spaces between the slats above her. Sporadic gunshots, thuds of falling bodies, animalistic roars, shouting voices, frightened and agonized screams were a distorted, muffled symphony. The girl knew where she was going and dragged herself on bent elbows and knees through the soil steadily deeper into the crawlspace.

Then she saw the eyes. Red. Glittering. Hundreds of them like tiny coals in the thick choking smoke. Pilar froze in terror, gagging from the rank, suffocating fumes of the close atmosphere. A horrible furry sea of rats came squealing and scrambling in an undulating rancid carpet out of the gloom at her, crawling all over her pinned body as she helplessly screamed, utterly hysterical. Then the rats were gone. They had been fleeing in stampeding panic, not attacking.

Gasping in relief under the planks, she was almost about to move when she heard the wings. A vast, fluttering curtain of squeaking vampire bats surged out of the inky smoke-filled darkness in a storm cloud of flapping wings, jeweled eyes, sharp teeth and skeletal claws. The airborne rodents hit Pilar like a tidal wave as she screamed hysterically all over again, covering her head as the flood of bats washed over her. Then they, too, beat a hasty retreat.

Gripped with fear and fighting tears, Pilar finally reached her destination. A trap door directly over her. Footfalls on the floorboards above. "It is me, Pilar! Let me up."

Her mother's voice responded. "Pilar!"

"Mama it is me, open the hatch!"

GGRRRRRRRRRRRRRRRRRRR . . .

Pilar froze at the low growl, nearby. Two glowing red eyes, not bat or rat but big as plates, shone in the dark. It was what the vermin were fleeing. The gigantic hungry werewolf was down in the crawlspace with her. The bristly spine of its unnatural back crammed into the tight space rubbed along the planks above as it pulled itself out of the gloom on its big thick paws with a steady *scrape scrape scrape*. Its fanged jaws snapped at the air, tongue lolling, nostrils flaring. The monster's progress was slow but relentless.

"Open the hatch, Mama! Hurry!" Pilar cried desperately.

Above her, many hands fumbled with the latch and threw it open. She gripped the pistol in both fists and fired twice into the darkness between the red saucers. One of them went dark as she shot an eye out. The savage creature howled in berserk high-pitched agony and pounced at her. Just as the hatch was flung open, the girl leapt upward, bare feet leaving the dirt ground under the church just as a hairy tree trunk of an arm and shovel of a talon raked at dead air where she had lain an instant before.

Leaping up through the trap door, Pilar landed on both feet safely on the wooden floorboards of the small back room, catching her balance as the guns clattered to the ground, surrounded by the people of the village who had been imprisoned in the room. Her townsmen slammed the hatch shut and locked it. Quickly, the girl took her pistol in a two-handed grip like Tucker taught her and pumped a full load of bullets through the floorboards at the unseen creature pounding on the locked hatch. The planks kicked up splintered wood as the slugs thudded holes into them. Underneath, the wounded maddened creature wailed in dismal anguish but still beat on the floor in its weakened state.

"I knew you would come."

Pilar turned breathlessly to see Bonita standing facing her, her little sister's eyes bright and tearful.

"I promised I would come back for you, little one, didn't I?" Overjoyed, Pilar set down her weapons and swept Bonita up in her arms, hugging her in blessed relief and gratefully kissing the girl's face and head. Brushing away the child's filthy hair, the girl looked her over, checking for injuries. "Are you alright, Bonita, did they hurt you, were you scared?"

Bonita smiled like sunlight and shook her head vigorously. "I wasn't scared, not really, because you always keep your promises."

"*Bueno.*"

Now the gunfire was growing more clamorous in the chapel next door and Pilar set Bonita down for there was much to do to get everyone out of there alive. Her vow to her sister was unfulfilled as yet.

"*Mi hija.*" Having almost forgotten about her, Pilar choked back tears at the sight of her mother's wrinkled, beaming, sobbing face. The little old woman embraced her joyfully and the other villagers hugged Pilar with great relief that she was alive. She kissed and clenched hands with a few, then shook them off, reloading her pistol with silver bullets. "I have brought men. We have made silver bullets for our guns to kill the werewolves. But we must hurry. Make haste, my friends."

"What do we do?" Her mother trembled.

"While they fight them and kill them," her daughter replied, "we go out the back way and take the horses."

More roars came from below as another werewolf joined the first one beneath the floorboards, blocking their retreat. The crowd of unarmed villagers exchanged fearful glances. The boards below their feet shook and began to crack from the onslaught of claws below, trying to get at them.

"So now we make a different plan." Pilar shrugged.

She passed out the guns.

Inside the church, the cowboy gunfighters engaged the monsters in a pitched battle.

"Get those people the hell out of here!" Tucker yelled to Bodie as he cranked off shot after shot with his Winchester rifle at the wall of hair, fangs and claws. Fix gave his buddy cover as Bodie leapt over the pews, scrambling across the burning alter. The big Swede could already hear the muffled screams and cries for help from the trapped villagers inside the back room. He leapt onto the tabernacle. Reaching the door, he crisscrossed his arms, firing the pistols in opposite directions, smoothly shooting two werewolves coming at him on either side straight through the heart. The two beasts fell, swiftly transforming back into men and were quickly devoured by three wolfmen resembling eight-foot-tall fiery torches. The stench of burning fur and rank canine flesh choked the cowboy as he jerked back the wooden beam bolting the door and flung it wide.

A flood of grateful peasants poured out of the room like a tidal wave of water from a burst dam. Bodie held them back but the people froze in their tracks when they got an eyeful of the spectacular horrific tableau of the fiery church swarming with werewolves that blocked their way.

"Give 'em guns and ammo!" yelled Tucker.

Fix was already on it, grabbing a belt of silver bullets and shoving them into the waiting hands of the villagers. He grabbed an armload of rifles and pistols from the bandits' weapons stockpile and dumped them on the altar. The peasants swiftly took up arms and grabbed fistfuls of silver bullets and stuffed them in the breeches and cylinders of the firearms. The naked women, the fight back in them, also brandished weapons. Sweat glistened on their bare heaving breasts.

"Shoot for the hearts! *El Corazon*! *El Corazon*!" Tucker shouted, gesturing to them, and put a round square into the left side of a rampaging wolfman, dropping it in its tracks, to demonstrate.

The Mexicans crossed themselves in awe as they saw the corpse go from beast to man but then they got busy shooting werewolves. Pilar stood in front of the others, firing her pistol in a two-handed grip. The air filled with gunfire as bullets screamed and ricocheted and caromed. Fangs and claws and fur flew. All was chaos. A final battle of good and evil was taking place as side by side the gunslingers fought with the villagers as one army, making a last stand, delivering the seemingly relentless hordes of werewolves to perdition. They fired until their guns were empty, hammers clicking uselessly on spent chambers. They were out of silver bullets.

More monsters reared out of the flames. Forced back, the humans retreated to the vestibule. The creatures blocked their escape through the front doors of the church and advanced on them, enraged.

Then Tucker saw it on the floor.

A last canvas ammo belt filled with silver bullet cartridges.

The cowboy leapt forward and picked it up, falling back into the huddled group of his fellow gunfighters and the villagers cornered in the nave. Even though he had the ammo belt, he knew in the time it would take them to reload their guns, the werewolves would tear them asunder.

So the cowboy pulled his arm back and heaved the last ammunition belt as hard as he could at the wolfman leading the pack.

The creature caught it in his talons.

It was the beast whose eyes Tucker recognized as Mosca, the bandit leader. Its black rubbery lips pulled back in a drooling leer over the rows of bloody fangs as it held up the ammo belt as if to display it in triumph. Flames licked across the fur of its arms but it paid them no notice.

The other ten werewolves stomped forward through the burning pews, their paws collapsing the cindered wood in showers of sparks and timber as the creatures gathered to the right and left of the leader of the pack. Mosca threw his snout back and roared savagely, clenching the canvas strap lined with silver slugs.

The werewolves did not see that the canvas belt had caught on fire.

Flames were licking the metal casings, turning them red hot . . .

Just like Tucker planned.

He winked at Bodie and Fix.

"Get down!" The three gunslingers shouted in warning as they jumped up and dragged the villagers behind the altar, shielding the peasants with their bodies.

PAPAPAPAPAPAPKAKAKAKAKAKAPAPAPAPAPKAKAKA-KAOW!

The air was rent with deafening gunfire, as every single one of the seventy-five silver bullets in the burning ammo belt held in the wolf-man's paw fired in staccato sequence like a string of firecrackers going off, slugs flying in every direction, the rounds peppering the were-wolves and making them dance spastically. Bloody eruptions like red flowers blossomed in their heads, arms, legs and stomachs.

And hearts.

With final despairing yelps of defiance and pain, the remaining werewolves dropped dead, crumpling onto the incinerated pews and floor of the immolating chapel.

As their bodies returned to human form, the flames cremated the corpses until all was ash.

The Men Who Walk Like Wolves walked no more.

The people raised their guns and cheered.

The open doors to the church lay open, beckoning out to the bright, moonlit, fresh night air and safety. There wasn't much time. The gunfighters and villagers saw Santa Sangre was coming down on their heads. Pieces of the roof fell in burning piles of torched timber.

"Go!" The gunslingers grabbed the villagers and hauled them through the smoldering aisles, ducking the fiery debris raining down and exploding in showers of flame and sparks all about them. The people plunged headlong through the open doors of the church and they ran and fell and tumbled down the hill. Behind their fleeing figures, the roof and parapet of the spire of Santa Sangre collapsed in on itself and the blazing steeple crashed to earth.

The heavy mission bell hit the ground and sounded in a last single ringing gong that sang over the town and the desert, echoing across the land.

The only silver left was one bullet in the chamber of Tucker's gun.

In the final hours before dawn, the gunfighters had scoured the rubble of the church, searching in vain for the slugs they'd slammed in the hearts of the werewolves, but the bandits were ash and unaccountably so were the silver bullets that killed them. Bodie said it didn't make any damn sense. Fix said it was just part of a whole lot of things that didn't make any damn sense and never would.

"You win some you lose some," Tucker said.

Tired, wounded and downhearted, the three gunfighters trod down the hill. The whole village stood waiting for them. The gratitude and respect in their faces sobered the gunfighters, who watched as the men and women bowed. The peasant girl who had first walked up to them the day before and brought them here with promises of silver now bid them farewell with no silver, yet something of greater value.

"You are men of true honor. There is no price to this or measure of our people's thankfulness," Pilar spoke softly. "We will never forget you and your legend will be told by our children's children."

"Hell, we didn't have nothing better to do," said Tucker. He stood before Pilar and in her loving eyes saw home, but he knew he couldn't stay. He wanted to say something but he couldn't, yet in her steady gaze he saw she understood, had before they ever met, that this was how it was supposed to be and everything was all right now. Time to part.

The villagers brought the gunslingers their horses and saddles and the big men mounted up. The entire village watched the men go. As the three cowboys rode to the top of the ridge, they were bathed in rosy dawn light.

Pilar stood in front of the other villagers, her beatific face whipped by the wind, features shining with love and pride and rewarded faith to last a dozen lifetimes as she watched her heroes ride off into destiny.

She touched her belly and smiled.

Up on the ridge, the men sat in their saddles wearily, looking behind them down into the valley. Santa Sangre lay in ashes, but the tiny figures of the villagers were already sifting through the smoking rubble, like ants on a dirt hole.

Fix shook his head. "They're rebuildin' the damn church. Don't got money to eat but looks to me like they already puttin' it back up again." He took a pull of the bottle of whisky and tossed it to Bodie, who had a swig and chucked the bottle to Tucker.

Opening his gloved fist, Tucker held out the last silver bullet that was all that remained of the treasure. "This silver wouldn't buy us a drink, boys," he spit. "We're as broke as when we rode in."

"Somebody had to kill them son of a bitches. They had it coming," stated Fix.

"Boys, we done some bad stuff before, maybe we'll do bad again, but today we're the good guys. It's a damn good feeling," said Bodie.

They all smiled at one another, nodding. "Good deeds could get to be a bad habit," added Tucker ironically.

"So what we gonna do about you, Tucker?" said Fix, indicating his fellow gunslinger's bandaged shoulder. "You got bit. That means you're gonna turn into one of those werewolves."

"Don't know if it was a bite, mebbe it could have been a scratch, I disremember." Tucker eyed his companions with a wry glint in his eye. "Reckon I got a month before the next full moon and you boys find out." He eyed the lone silver bullet in his hand then chucked it to Fix, who caught it. "Which case, you'll know what to do with this."

"We're friends until then."

"Until then."

They laughed, their friendly voices carrying across the rough badlands.

The Guns of Santa Sangre rode off.

ERIC RED IS A LOS ANGELES BASED NOVELIST, SCREEN-writer, and film director. His first two novels, a dark coming-of-age tale about teenagers called *Don't Stand So Close* and a dark fantasy called *The Guns of Santa Sangre* are available from SST Publications. His other two novels, a science fiction thriller called *It Waits Below*, and a mystery crime thriller called *White Knuckle*, are available from Crossroad Press. His fifth novel *The Wolves of El Diablo*, the sequel to *The Guns of Santa Sangre*, will be published in hardcover, trade paperback and digital editions by SST Publications in August 2017. Mr. Red directed and wrote the films *Cohen and Tate* for Hemdale, *Body Parts* for Paramount, *Undertow* for Showtime, *Bad Moon* for Warner Bros. and *100 Feet* for Grand Illusions Entertainment. His original screenplays include *The Hitcher* for TriStar, *Near Dark* for DeLaurentiis Entertainment Group, *Blue Steel* for MGM and *The Last Outlaw* for HBO. His recent published horror and suspense short stories have been in *Cemetery Dance* magazine, *Weird Tales* magazine, *Shroud* magazine, *Dark Delicacies III: Haunted* anthology, *Dark Discoveries* magazine, Mulholland Books' Popcorn Fiction, among others. He created and wrote the sci-fi/horror comic series and graphic novel *Containment* from SST Publications and the horror western comic series *Wild Work* for Antarctic Press. Visit his website at www.ericred.com.

CPSIA information can be obtained
at www.ICGtesting.com
Printed in the USA
BVOW03*1549270617
487599BV00001B/2/P